HEAR AND ANSWER ME!

by Ronald Joseph Tocchini

www.trafford.com

North America & international
toll-free: 1 888 232 4444 (USA & Canada)
phone: 250 383 6864 ✦ fax: 812 355 4082

This work is dedicated to Mary Wineberg, my neighbor and dear friend who helped me with the technological aspects of preparing the work for submission. Thank you.

I would also like to acknowledge the cover artist, my nephew and godson Jon Robert Tocchini.

Hear and Answer Me!

B ATS, A FLURRY of them, were flying aimlessly through an indeterminate area of the troposphere. Undetectable, due to a lingering darkness and some occult faculty of their own, their presence could nonetheless be felt by everyone thereabout as they fluttered and swished through a cool but balmy air. At the same time, crickets in a crop of cornstalks creaked, while bullfrogs belched at the banks of a nearby canal.

Waters of the canal gurgled like those of a swollen brook in spring. Furthermore, their ripply waves, which flowed in the manner in which one writes, glistened in the glimmer of a waning-stellar glow. Said waters were ebullient as well, and thus, their waves very lively licked and lapped that canal's impacted banks.

An odor, moreover, one which likened to that of unkempt cages in a zoo, permeated the ambiance and generated an effluvium, one that was indicative of neglect and decay.

Along furrows where the crop of cornstalks was rooted, a pack of raccoons lumbered about. Dodging dumps of dung and puddles of urine, the burly beasts scoured a rugose ground. Oblivious to the miasma that emanated from the foregoing waste, they focused on making a final round for viands before darkness would surrender to dawn. Busily, therefore, they ventured from the furrows to the canal. Thither, they washed their findings before consuming them one by one.

Suddenly, two of the coons vied over viands, and, growing increasingly vexed by the moment, they eventually began to brawl. Soon, other coons joined in the altercation, and before very long, there was total mayhem in the midst of the crop of tall, gangly stalks. Like ferocious pitbulls, the brawling coons battled. Indeed, they viciously attacked, hacked, smacked, and clawed! Furthermore, they sometimes sunk incisors in flesh, and, employing the canines as well, they tore away the flesh from tendons, ligaments, cartilage, and bone!

While the combative coons brawled, their sizeable bodies unavoidably crashed into stalks. Jostling the latter with no slight fury, they alarmed many creatures that resided therein. Insects, for instance, namely spiders and scorpions or even little black widows, scurried frenetically over shank-like stems and spiraled sheathes for leaves. Moreover, in silky tufts of fleshy ears, squirmy worms wiggled while issuing therefrom. Meanwhile, around tassels, which tipped the tops of the tall stalks, bewildered bees hovered. Confounded by the ruckus, they persistently surrounded the tassels, but, daunted by the trauma that was caused by the coons, they remained hesitant to land. Sparrows, in the meantime, nestled in niches where ears sprouted from the stalks' stems, also reacted to the violent intrusion. Frantically, they flapped their little swept wings, and, abandoning their cover, they took to flight.

Overhead, in a sky colored royal blue, heavenly bodies glimmered. Faint was their glimmer, since the incipient light of a nascent dawn was presently causing them to wane. Hence, they would soon fade and disappear from view.

The agitated birds convened at an altitude that was well above the crop from which they had flown. Quickly, now, they aligned themselves in a characteristic V-shape pattern, and without delay, they ventured in the direction of the early morning's glow.

Daybreak's incipient gleam unveiled the summits of a huge *cordillera*. Jagged like the cutting edge of a lumberjack's saw, those mountaintops sketched a daunting silhouette on a sky of reddish gold. Lofty as well, they towered over a valley, which, emerging in the early light of day, displayed an enormous area. This was cradled between the foregoing *cordillera* and its counterpart to the west. The airborne flock of sparrows availed themselves of the growing coruscation in order to examine the valley floor. Eager to find a haven in which to safely land, they kept eyes focused downward and viewed what is described hereinbelow.

Tassels of an amber coloration were beginning to glimmer. Tipping the tops of a trillion stalks, they carpeted an unending maze of verdure, which, apportioned into multi-acre plots, resembled a magnificent quilt of neatly sewn patches. The plots were separated from each other by virtue of dirt access roads that bordered every one of them on all four sides. Each access road was flanked by a waterway of a sort. Most of these were irrigation ditches; some, deeply dug canals. The latter, which were fewer in number, brought a constant supply of water from wetter lands in the north. The ditches, on the other hand, were flooded only during moments of irrigation.

The observant birds maintained their eastbound course and crossed high above a paved highway. This highway, running down the valley's center, articulated towns in the south with those in the north. Abandoned at that early hour, it appeared desolate, eerie, and somewhat surreal.

Not having yet found a favorable spot in which to alight, the viewing fowl raised their sights a bit and peered in the direction of a nascent sun, which, beginning to creep from behind the huge *cordillera,* radiated beams to galaxies that were beyond the scope of anyone's sight. Ubiquitous, moreover, the radiance additionally brightened the crops and mountains as well.

The forlorn sparrows hurried toward the *cordillera* like wandering seabirds that, having lost their bearings and gone astray, hasten to an island on the open sea. Upon arriving at the valley's east end, the flock of fowl decided to gain altitude. Evidently, they were planning to explore the *cordillera's* foothills. However, shortly after initiating the ascent, they became distracted by something on the land below them. What met their eyes was an irregularity in the order of things, and it demanded their undivided attention causing them to halt in midair. Then, while breaking formation for the time being, they hovered over what their eyes had seen.

An esplanade of sun-bleached dunes hugged the *sierra's* base, and thus, they resembled a beach, the kind that is found on the unending coastline of some tropical isle. Furthermore, similar to the way in which a beach slopes to a sea's sandy shore, the esplanade's rolling dunes sloped gradually to the bank of a water-filled canal.

On the dunes, at a spot not far from where they met the *sierra's* base, was a sight for the perusing birds to behold. Shanty-like shacks, twelve of them, marred the esplanade's eucharistic whiteness. Strewn haphazardly over an area of about a hundred yards square or more, they called to mind the dreary looking barracks of a detainee camp, the kind that were used during the Second World War.

The airborne bunch became intrigued by what they had perceived, and, motivated by their curiosity, they decided to explore. Therefore, they immediately returned to their regular flight formation. Next, careening to the right, they completed a half circle before alighting at a spot that was about thirty yards from the nearest of the twelve shacks. With claws planted firmly on sand, the birds maintained their original V-shaped pattern. Moreover, their actions were performed in unison. For example, before advancing, they all glanced to the right to observe the *cordillera 's* base. Next, all of them peeked, as a group, to their left. Peering in that direction and down a bit, they focused on the nearside bank of the water-filled canal.

Assured of their safety, the cautious birds then advanced toward the group of shacks like a colony of ants crawling to the top of a sandy slope. After proceeding forward for several moments, the ambulant birds halted in front of the shack that was nearest to the spot where they had alighted. Turning to their right, the observant bunch viewed the structure from its front side and noticed that it was not much bigger than a two-horse stable. It seemed particularly diminutive, moreover, when viewed against the huge *cordillera's* base. Regarding its general appearance, let us note that it was a sight to behold.

Paltry and squalid, the shack was a typical shanty, of the kind that was once found in the camptowns of the Old South. Indeed, it belched with poverty and neglect. Nevertheless, it was of interest to the forlorn flock, who were so desirous of a haven to have for their own. Curious to attain a more inclusive view, they therefore began to circle the structure in clockwise fashion.

While circling the hut, the inquisitive fowl tended to gravitate toward it. Attentive, they carefully listened for signs of life that might emanate from within. Sounds of snoring, farting, panting, and sighing met each bird's senses. Intrigued by what they heard, all of them focused more intensively on the hut, particularly on the areas whencefrom the sounds had come. Perusing the structure, they saw that which follows.

The shanty's sides consisted of plain wooden planks of pine, which, having been arranged vertically, were held together by two-by-fours. These, nailed diagonally thereupon, extended from upper corner to lower corner on each of the structure's four sides. Planks and two-by-fours were visibly weather-beaten. Indeed, bleached by a torrid desert's rays and sandblasted by *scirocco*-like winds, the wood's surface appeared desiccated like the texture of dried cornstalks. Regarding the condition of the roof, one could safely assume that, given the overall squalor of the structure, it probably left much to be desired as a protection from the elements.

Having circled the shack, the perusing bunch of fowl now convened at its front side once more. Thither, they stayed and stared at the entrance, as if waiting for someone to open the door.

Eager were they to enter the abode in order to discover and to thoroughly explore.

After a moment or so, rusty hinges squeaked a bit as the foregoing door moved slowly to and slightly fro. Then, said door remained slightly ajar. A crack, narrow but noticeable, had evinced itself. Thither and downward, at about a foot and a half from a sandy floor, a pair of nostrils appeared. Wedged in the opening to which we have alluded, the nostrils were observed to be dripping some snot. Moreover, while shining in the daylight, they visibly wrinkled at the end of a snout. The latter, having already protruded, soon pointed upward, and thus, the creature sniffed for scents in the balmy morning air. Then, wedging its snout very noticeably, the animal nudged the door and caused it to open at ninety degrees. Accordingly, the body of the beast became visible.

At the threshold, the animal now stood. It remained still while keeping all fours planted firmly on said sandy floor. Its eyes, one on each side of the elongated snout, peered at the V-shaped flock of perusing birds. The animal's ears, floppy like those of a beagle, drooped from the head, which was obviously the head of a hound.

For a while, dog and birds remained motionless; however, when the former began to advance toward the latter, these receded like a wave recedes after it has covered the sand at the shore of a following sea.

Having retreated for about five yards, the sparrows came to a sudden halt. Keeping their sights on the intrusive beast, they saw it turn to its right and trot toward a nearby well. After advancing for six or seven yards, the dog stopped to sniff the ground. This pause allowed the wary fowl to study the animal some more. What the peeping birds saw was a short-haired hound of a brownish coloration. Lengthwise, it measured about two and a half feet. Its height was about a foot and a half, from the ground to the spine. Being skinny, its ribcage protruded and thereby resembled the keyboard of a xylophone. Moreover, the legs were sinewy and stiff, like those of a greyhound.

After sniffing the ground, the hungry-looking hound resumed its brusque pace and trotted to the aforementioned well. Having arrived, it brought its left flank alongside the well's wall of stone, and, lifting the leg in a characteristic manner, it urinated thereupon. The dog's tail, which resembled that of a possum's, remained in an upward position and thereby facilitated the process of urination. Such a position or posture revealed a tight rump and a scrotum. Drooping, the latter hung dingle-dangle and jiggled synchronously with the movements of the hound's unsteady body.

Having relieved himself, the hound lowered his left leg and brought it to its former position. While remaining stationery for a brief period of time, he sniffed the well's wall, precisely the area which he had recently christened with his waste. Moments later, he quickly motioned to his right, and, after completing a half circle, he began to walk across the dunes, directly toward the nearside bank of the aforementioned canal. Thirsty, due to dehydration and a seasonal incandescence, he panted while dragging his tongue along the warming sand.

While trudging resolutely over the esplanade, the beast suddenly came to a halt when he perceived the clangor of a vehicle's engine. Remaining still, he raised his head and peered straight ahead, down a dirt access road. The following is what he saw.

Approaching with no little haste and a considerable fury, a red-colored pickup truck was bouncing on humps and bumps while zig-zagging over the road's irregular crown. Its tires left a murky cloud of dust which visibly cluttered the air and rained on stalks, particularly ones that lined the ditches on each side of the dirt-packed road.

The startled dog stared at the vehicle's windshield, as if trying to identify the driver. Unsuccessful was his attempt, however, because the glass sparkled in the brilliance of the risen sun and dazzled him significantly. Notwithstanding the impediment, the animal still managed to monitor the truck's movements by examining its shell.

The truck's radiator screen, which was located between two glassy headlights, measured about two and a half feet square. Behind the latter, the engine's fan churned incessantly, and thereby it seemed to be drawing dust and pollutants that were plaguing the air. A rather large hood displayed ventilated ribs on each of its sides. Said ribs were visibly exhaling the pulverulence which was being inhaled by the screen. Fenders, one on each side of the vehicle's hood, bore the two headlights mentioned above. These, laden with dirt and smattered with bodies of dead insects, were glassy but not shiny. A front bumper, bent and dented at various points along its tarnished frame, served as evidence of frequent use, of no slight abuse, and of definite neglect. The radiator screen, when viewed in conjunction with the hood, fenders, headlights and bumper, bore a semblance to the visage of a gigantic beetle, one that was formicating along a path between two fields of tall grass.

The dog, meanwhile, had become agitated by the intrusion. As a result, he aggressively approached the canal's bank that was closer to him. Thither, he capered to and fro, as well as from side to side while barking persistently at the forthcoming vehicle which, in the interim, was nearing the waterway's far side bank.

The road on which the pickup truck was traveling led to the one that ran parallel to the canal. Upon arriving at that junction, the vehicle first crossed a dry irrigation ditch via a makeshift bridge, and then it swerved recklessly to its right. So sharp was the turn that it almost seemed as if the truck was going to roll over and fall into the waterway's stream. After careening in the manner described, the truck raced for another twenty-five yards or so. Then, the wheels locked. As a result, the vehicle's body skidded and slid for another ten yards before coming to a sudden halt. Still, it now stayed positioned alongside the aforementioned canal.

Enveloped in a cloud of dust, one which had been generated by the whirling of its wheels, the pickup truck was currently imperceptible to the eyes of the viewing hound. This condition caused his combative behavior to abate. Noiseless and motionless, he stood staring intensely in the direction of the pulverous veil that concealed the machine's shell of steel.

Cloaked in a smoke-like cloud, the truck remained hidden from sight for a while. In such a state it stayed, since wind was very scarce in the valley during that current time of the year. Nonetheless, the dust did eventually settle. Hence, the vehicle slowly emerged like an abandoned boat might emerge amidst the rising fog of a misty sea.

As a result of the truck's reappearance, the watchful hound proceeded to bark, caper, and jump near the canal's bank.

The pickup truck measured about eighteen feet in length. Typical of the kind that is employed in many American farms, it showed signs of wear and tear. We have already observed some neglect on the vehicle's front bumper, and we'll now note that the shell, as well, evidenced no slight remiss. For example, on the side that was visible to its viewer, smatterings of dung and dark-colored mud had collected and caked. Flung there by churning, tractor-like tires, said smatterings smeared and marred that portion of the shell's reddish tint and thereby converted that color into one of tawny brown.

Keeping eyes fixed on the stalled machine, the clamorous canine soon zeroed in on the window of the driver's side. Brief was the glance, however, since he again became dazzled by the sun's reflection on glass. Then, moments later, he saw that the window was being lowered and, within seconds, the perusing beast managed to peer into the vehicle's cab area in order to see if he could identify the driver. Nevertheless, the view was opaque, since the cab's roof shaded much of the daylight and thereby prevented a pellucid view.

The barking beast displayed a remarkable tenacity in his attempt to discover the intruder and to intimidate through aggressive harassment. What persistence! How unrelentingly ferocious he appeared! Moreover, praiseworthy was his desire to faithfully defend his turf. However, something alarming now transpired. It was an occurrence that would fill any viewer with awe.

At the open window space, on the truck driver's side, the gun barrel of a twelve-gauge shotgun suddenly appeared. Protruding thencefrom, its purplish bluing glistened in the matinal brilliance. Moving slightly up and down, as well as from side to side, it seemed to indicate that the bearer of that arm was coordinating peep and rear sights for the purpose of an accurate aim. Shifting and repositioning in the manner described hereinabove, the weapon's cannon bore a semblance to the kind that is mounted on an army tank's swiveling top.

The vigilant canine quickly cowered upon viewing the gunbarrel that was aimed at his head. Accordingly, all barking abated, and even the animal's yelping was soon just a whimper. Querulously, the humbled hound then growled as he groveled and cringed with no slight fright. Moreover, lowering his head, he peered downward at the ground, like a sacrificial goat prepares for its slaughter. Meekened so, he remained submissive, until... *Bam!!*

A whizbang of buckshot all but annihilated the humbled one. What a truculent sight! How sanguinary the mess! Let us pause here for a moment to picture the scene. Imagine mangled bits of the dog's body parts scattered amidst scarlet-colored blotches of blood. All of that stained an area of sun-bleached sand, the same area which the valiant beast had so tenaciously attempted to defend.

The flock of sparrows, by the way, the ones which had remained near the aforementioned well, had also been in the line of fire. As a result, many of them had become maimed by stray shot, and as a result, they frenetically fluttered about on the sand like chickens flutter after having been recently decapitated. The other sparrows, ones that had remained unscathed, quickly rose and took to flight. Panic stricken, each of them flew in a different direction and subsequently disappeared from view.

Meanwhile, about three hundred feet above the truculent scene we have recently observed, a flock of vultures loomed. Gliding and careening, soaring then coasting, they sailed through the balmy air like flown kites float in the flush of a breezy spring day. Moreover, while circling persistently over the foregoing scene, the predators remained focused thereon and perused every detail that met their eyes.

The shanties, all twelve of them, quaked as occupants therein very audibly bustled from beds to front doors. The latter soon swung open with no slight fury, and at each threshold stood a naked Mexican man. Alarmed by the gunshot, each man had abandoned the warmth of his mate's tender body in order to seek a cause for the disturbance. Perplexed, every one of them advanced a step or two from the threshold and, shading their eyes with both hands, peered straight ahead in the direction whence the shot had come. Motionless, all stood gazing in the light of the new day's sun and under the scrutiny of the overhead buzzards who perused the men one by one. The following is what those birds observed.

Each man's stature and build appeared somewhat enhanced when compared to the meager size of his humble abode. However, objectively speaking, all of the men tended to be rather diminutive and lean. Regarding their complexions, they were swarthy, and hence, they blended well with the paltry-darkish aspect of the huts' general exteriors. Hair, black and greasy, covered every man's scalp and the nape of the neck, too. Eyes of a midnight darkness, separated by a slightly snubbed nose, were almond shaped. This characteristic, together with that of high cheekbones, evidenced a trace of indigenous origin. A moustache and sideburns, slight but noticeable, revealed a certain concern for the *macho* look. Speaking of the latter, all of the men seemed well endowed with a sizeable penis. Being uncircumcised, the extra flap of foreskin added a dimension or two to that organ. This, by the way, was semi-erected on some of the men, which was a condition that told a bold tale of recent sexual activity. Cocked and somewhat bent, the shape bore a semblance to the neck, head and face of a hen, one that was gawking from a frizzy nest wherein lay two tepid eggs.

Within the shanties, plaintive wails from babies drowned all sounds of the surroundings. The little ones, frightened by the commotion, craved to be consoled by their mothers. The latter, meanwhile, who were in the nude like their male counterparts, bustled about from bed to crib. Taking their infants and cradling them, they each muffled all wails by stuffing a tiny mouth with a crimson-colored nipple, one of two. Each of the latter capped a pair of supple breasts.

While nursing, the women never turned their eyes away from the thresholds of their abodes. Worried about the safety of their families, every one of them tenaciously admonished her partner who remained peering near the shanty's front door.

Gazing straight ahead and slightly down, all twelve men watched the wounded sparrows agonize. Expressions of repugnance grew on every man's countenance upon seeing the crippled creatures frantically flounder on the sandy dunes. Flipping and flapping in such a spasmodic manner, the inflicted fowl likened to fish that are caught in the web of a fisherman's net. Exposed to air, those creatures of the sea very lively flip, flap, and flounder on decks and in hatches of seagoing crafts. Meanwhile, their bellow-like gills rhythmically expand and contract as they desperately crave oxygen from water. The lack of it, one well knows, eventually causes them to gasp and to choke before they shutter and finally expire.

Disturbing to us is the experience of watching a creature hopelessly fight for its life. Hence, upsetting was the sight of the afflicted birds to the men described above. However, the scene of those agonizing fowl proved only somewhat gruesome to the viewing group when compared to that of the dead dog's body parts. Disgusted, indeed, the twelve individuals became at the sight of that animal's remains! Such remains, we recall, lay scattered amidst splotches of blood. The latter had already been blotted by a granular surface of sun-bleached sand.

Sentiments of disgust and abomination grew as the gazing Mexicans noticed the pickup truck that remained parked alongside the canal's far side bank. Rancor now took hold of them, because they associated the vehicle with a well-known *bête noire* with whom they all were familiar. We shall understand the reason for such a deep resentment when we study the person who, having opened the vehicle's door, sat sideways at the edge of the driver's seat. After spitting a wad of snuff into the canal, he faced downward and examined the ground where his feet were about to land.

A bald, waxy scalp, that of the driver, shined in the matinal brilliance as he issued from the truck's cab. Holding the shotgun in a present arms position, he let his torso slide from the seat like a walrus slides from a solid rock's top while returning to the depths of an ocean or sea. The man quickly planted a pair of worn wrangler boots firmly in the sand near the vehicle's running board. Thither, he stood cradling the shotgun at midsection. Leaning back against the portion of the seat whence he had slid, he supported his corpulent mass. This filled a long-sleeved khaki shirt and a pair of shabby Levis, like ground gristle and meat all stuffed into an intestine that is used as sausage wrap.

Gazing straight ahead then, the driver revealed himself to his viewers. What a hideous sight to behold! Ears, floppy like the pinnae on an elephant fetus, mushroomed from a massive head, which we have noted was bald. Cheeks, reddish and porky, bulged on both sides of a potato-shaped nose. Lips, moistened by frequent spurts of spittle, now puckered to spit another wad of snuff into the canal's southbound stream. A chin, tripled by rolls of blubber, jiggled when shaken, like the throat of a pecking rooster or buzzard cock.

A closer look at the man's face revealed his eyes. Cold-blue and somewhat bloodshot, the latter were beady and venomous, too. Demoniac, they evidenced a capacity for a wicked viciousness, like the hysterical-looking eyes of a famished bird of prey, one that is prone to strip and feed on the entrails of some helpless creature.

Having spat, the driver now eyeballed the twelve Mexicans one by one. Then, taking his shotgun, he grabbed the grip with his right hand and placed the palm of his left under the wooden casing that was midway between the trigger and the barrel's tip. Next, jamming the stock's butt end in his right armpit, he held the weapon in a firing position. Finally, he activated the pump-action device by using his extended left hand to quickly slide, to and fro, the wooden casing which housed it. *Shuck-shuck! Plop!*

The foregoing activation resulted in ridding the firing chamber of an emptied cartridge and replacing it with a loaded one.

The high-flying vultures winced at the shotgun's **shuck-shuck** sound and the *plop* that ensued. Wary, all of them were, and thus, they seemed particularly conditioned to prepare themselves at the slightest hint of any peril.

After wincing, each one of the fowl flapped its pair of condor-like wings. Gaining altitude, they all distanced themselves from the gun's range of fire. While they hovered way above the scene below, those birds' blackness glistened in the matinal glow. Meanwhile, each of them watched all activity that transpired.

Having aimed his gun in the general direction of all the twelve shanties, the gunman paused for a moment. Then, he raised the barrel's tip a bit, and, squeezing the trigger with his index finger, he fired a shot. *Bam!*

Daunting, indeed, was the whizzang that boomed! Terrifying, the pattern of pellets which o'er the roof of every hut zoomed! To the Mexican men, the message was unequivocally clear. Hence, abandoning their stances at the thresholds, each man promptly dashed back into his shack. Therein, not a one them wasted any time whatsoever. Fastidiously, they all gathered *huaraches,* a shirt, a *sombrero,* and trousers. Clothes in hand now, all twelve men abandoned their abodes, and, without taking time to dress, they darted toward the pickup truck where the menacing man impatiently awaited them.

A bird's eye view of the current scene revealed twelve scrambling men who, still in the nude, were frenetically forging across some sandy drifts. Hence, buttocks quaked while legs churned! Moreover, penises dangled and scrota jiggled as the men futilely attempted to sprint on a ground that gave! Trudging thereabout, they resembled ants, ones which, having recently absconded with viands, scurry as they ferry those findings to a sandy hill for a home.

The gunman, meanwhile, lowered his weapon, and, while holding it at waist level, he yelled at the top of his cigar-charred lungs, "*¡Ahndahlay, ahndahlay, heejoes day putah madray!*" The man's Spanish was severely limited to all sorts of blasphemous vulgarities, ones that he pronounced very badly. That which he meant to say was, "*¡Ándale, ándale, hijos de puta madre!*" The foregoing translates into vulgar English as, "Hurry up, hurry up, you sons of a mother whore!"

Having ululated in the manner depicted above, the crass man paused for a moment or so. Then, upon puckering his lips once more, he spat in the direction of the waterway's shore. This time, however, his wad of spittle landed not in the stream, but rather, it splattered on the flat surface of a thick wooden beam. Measuring about one foot wide, said beam extended from one bank to the other, a distance of about twenty-five feet. By doing so, it bridged the gap over that rushing stream of water. Serving that purpose, it would soon be traveled by that trudging bunch of twelve daunted men.

In single file, the incited dozen walked the plank, so to speak. Wary of the water that moved swiftly below them, each man gingerly measured every step he took as if walking a tightrope over perilous depths. Upon bridging the gap from bank to bank, the nimble group scurried to an area behind the pickup truck. Thither, not far from the vehicle's tailgate, all of them gathered and immediately began to dress.

Fidgeting, the men climbed into trousers and slipped into *huaraches* before fitting into shirts of mismatched sizes. Finally, a straw-woven *sombrero,* with which every individual capped his head, completed the indumentum of the typical Mexican peasant.

Each man was the characteristic *campesino,* that is to say, a man who worked the land every hour of the livelong day.

Having dressed, all twelve peasants huddled in an area off the truck's rear starboard. Arms akimbo, the men stood. Frowns, meanwhile, cracked on their bronze-colored faces, and their pearly whites sparkled in the early morning glow. Eyes, moreover, squinted in the sunlight. However, the daunted dozen dared not blink as they awaited a command from the feared fusilier.

Keeping his right hand on the gun's grip, and his left under the barrel, the gunman walked to the vehicle's rear. Next, he removed his right hand from said grip for a moment and reached for a catch on the truck's rear end. Tugging at it, he succeeded in releasing the tailgate. The latter clanked as it dropped down. Extending outward, it remained flush with the vehicle's bed.

The menacing man took two steps backwards and one to his right. Then, brandishing the gunbarrel, he motioned to the peasants to climb onto the foregoing bed. Peremptory was his demeanor, gruff his voice, as he yelled, *"¡Ahreebah, ahreebah, cheengonnays! ¡No may cheengare! ¡No poonyetear!*

The gunman was trying to say the following: *"¡Arriba, arriba, chingones! ¡No me chinguen! ¡No puñeteen!"* Translated into English, the foregoing means, "Get up, get up, you bunch of fuckers! Don't fuck with me! Don't jack off!"

Prodded by fear, the compliant crew stampeded to the pickup truck's rear. Wrestling with one another to see who would be first, they likened to livestock that, dying of thirst, vie for position at the trough.

After climbing onto the pickup truck's bed, each man claimed a spot to sit. Some stayed near the vehicle's back end; others, not far from its front. Like Indians at *a pow-wow,* all twelve men sat not facing the front or the sides, but to the vehicle's rear. In the meantime, they never took their eyes off the man with the gun.

Having corralled the peasants in the manner described hereinabove, the dreaded one advanced toward the tailgate. Freeing his right hand as he had done before, he used it to clasp the edge of said gate. Then, similar to a prison guard who closes a cell door, the man jerked the panel upward and caused it to slam shut once more. *Clank!*

The dreadful man gloated with glee while observing the fright in the peasant men's eyes. Supplicant, the men seemed to be begging for reprieve from an episode of terror and unspeakable grief.

While visually beseeching the inexorable man, the staring bunch promptly changed the direction of their glance. Instead of gazing into his eyes, they began to peer at an area that was about ten feet behind him and off to his right side. It was the area where the peasants had previously gathered to put on their clothes. What was it there that currently caught their sights? Let us see.

A peasant boy, dressed in the typical *campesino's* garb, stood staring from the spot where the daunted dozen had convened earlier. Slender and standing well over five feet in height, he was about average size for a Mexican boy in his early teens. A *sombrero,* the rim of which capped the parietal bone of that peasant boy's head, remained tilted back and thereby exposed his face to the day's growing light. This fact enabled the viewing crew to peruse him. The following is what they saw.

Curly locks, pitch black like the midnight hour, crept from under the hat's rim and unfurled onto the boy's bronze-colored brow. His nose, quasi flat like that of a mulatto, separated a pair of almond-shaped eyes, which were squinting as a result of their sensitivity to the sunlight's reflection on sand. The lad's eyebrows were ethereal, as if an able artist had gently dabbed them. Cheekbones, conspicuous and slightly raised, were rather lean but neither skinny nor elongated. Waxy-brown, they shined in the matinal glow. The youth's mouth, somewhat negroid like his nose, seemed disinclined to smile. His chin was dimpled slightly at the tip. It appeared neither pointed nor pudgy but rather just a little bit plump. Finally, a pair of pixie-like ears, the tips of which mushroomed out from the boy's coils of black hair, grazed the bottom sides of the *sombrero's* visor, and, being shapely, they complemented an aspect that was truly angelic.

A white shirt with long sleeves covered much of the peasant boy's torso. Said sleeves, which were excessively long, had been rolled up to a spot just above the wrists. The garment was buttonless, and, thus, it adhered to the boy's body by his having tied the two bottom front portions into one single clump of a knot at navel level. This created a V-shaped aperture which exposed a bronze-colored thorax. The latter shone in the morn's coruscation like the lad's waxy-brown cheeks and his brow, all of which we have already observed.

Trousers, white colored as well, were baggy and long. The pant legs, having been rolled up to ankle level, unveiled a pair of **huaraches**. The soles of those sandals consisted of strips of rubber from retread tires, ones that were tied to the youth's feet, by means of woven strands of rawhide.

The twelve gaping peasants sat in amazement, wondering about the newcomer's identity. Having gazed at him for quite some time, each man now turned his head and stared at the individual who was seated alongside him. Within moments, a conversation ensued between a few members of that bewildered brood!

"*Pero¿quién eh ese joven?*"

"*Yo no sé. No lo conozco.* "

"*Ni yo tampoco.*"

"*¿Qué chingada estaráh haciendo aquí?* "

"*¿Por qué no se lo preguntamos?* "

"*¡Ni modo! ¡No hay qu'enojarle al patrón! Puede que no le guste.*"

"*Buena idea, mano. Mejor no molestarle.*"

Questions and comments did indeed arise concerning the young stranger who seemed to have dropped from the sky.

The inquisitive bunch wanted to question the lad. However, they refrained from doing so out of fear of their *patron,* as they called him. Yes, he was their boss, and his crew well knew how he so zealously desired to maintain control over them. They were also well aware of how upset he could become when his dominion or authority was threatened.

At that time, the boss was becoming annoyed over the apparent disruption. Growing more impatient by the moment, he began to eyeball each and every man in the vocal brood as if seeking an explanation for said disruption. Meanwhile, a look of agitation on his fat face grew as he failed to restrain the members of the distracted crew. Flustered at not being able to hold their attention, the peeved *patron* decided to bludgeon them with another one of his crass remarks.

"*¡Kay passah, heejoes day putah madray askerosa?*"

The following is what the boss meant to say: "*¿Qué pasa, hijos de puta madre asquerosa?*"

In other words, "What's going on, sons of a disgusting mother whore?"

After demeaning his men, the blasphemous boss raised his gun a bit and pointed the barrel's tip at them.

Silent the crew again grew! Moreover, after having winced at the sight of the gunbarrel's tip, they cringed. Then, while peeping from under the visors of their wide-rimmed *sombreros,* they first cast eyes on the *patron.* Next, they ostensibly glimpsed at the newcomer who still stood in the same spot. Finally, the peering bunch glanced back at the boss. By repeatedly varying the direction of their glances in the foregoing manner, the groveling group seemed to be suggesting to the *patron* that he observe the area behind him and slightly off to his right.

While keeping both hands on the gun, the fat man now swung to his right. In doing so, he immediately laid eyes on the boy who had mysteriously shown up at the scene. This discovery caused him to growl: "What the fuck does this piss ant want?"

The peasant boy responded: "I am *Lazarillo.* I am looking for work. My father and older brother died in an accident. My family needs food and clothes."

The youngster barely uttered the last of his series of words when the boss exclaimed: "Well, wadaya know? An English-speakin' spic!"

Then, the man added: "Ain't no work here for a young pussy sniffer like yourself! This is man's work, boy. You otta be out sniffin girls' bicycle seats and jackin' off behind a tree! Ha, ha, ha!"

Rejected and dejected, the saddened lad dropped his head. While hanging it low, he kept arms and hands at his sides, and, standing still, he moved *not* from the spot where he stood. There he remained until the merciless man lashed out again.

"C'mon, boy! Get yur greasy ass outa here! Go pull yur little prick or go play with yur kid sister's pussy! I got work to do!"

Repudiated, the humbled boy raised his left forearm to his brow; and, using the sleeve of his shirt, he wiped away some tears. Then, turning to his right, he began to trod in the direction of a nearby crop of corn. To arrive at the edge of said crop, it was necessary for the lad to descend the road's shoulder and then cross the aforementioned irrigation ditch. Having done so, he slipped into the fronds of that crop via one of its millions of furrows, and, like a phantom, he vanished in a jungle of tall, leafy stalks.

Meanwhile, the mean boss had remained standing with his back to the pickup truck's tailgate. After watching the peasant boy walk away and drop out of sight, he swung back around in order to review his subdued brood.

Disconsolate about what they had recently witnessed, the melancholy crew of twelve seated men grew tearful. Moreover, penitent for having submissively countenanced such obnoxious behavior on the part of the *patron,* they felt ashamed and frustrated. Hence, full of sorrow and compunction, each of the men grieved in his own way and to himself. Feeling powerless, all of them peeped from under their straw-woven hats and sheepishly glanced at the gunman. Warily, they watched him and attempted to determine his next move. Listening, they heard him complain some more to himself.

"What in the fuck does that little needle dick think I'm runnin' here? A charitable organization? I'll be a son of a bitch if he can do a man's job! Shit, I'll bet his balls ain't even dropped yet!"

Having finished grumbling, the gun-toting boss motioned to his left. Taking a few steps, he rounded the vehicle's rear and then began walking back to its cab. On the way, he puckered his lips a bit once more and then spat a wad not near the truck but on the waterway's shore.

Once he arrived at the truck's front end, the beefy boss opened the driver's door and forced his fat mass into the cab. Thither he sat puffing and panting until he finally managed to catch his breath. Next, keeping both hands on the shotgun, he raised it overhead and swung it around to his right to an area just above the cab's rear window. There, he secured the weapon in place by wedging the gunbarrel and grip into two mounted, open-faced clamps.

Before starting the engine, the driver glanced straight ahead and then at about two o'clock into the vehicle's rearview mirror. What he now wanted to do was review his crew once more and to make sure they were not watching him. Reassured that things were under control, the wary boss now relaxed; and, while doing so, he allowed his imagination to drift. Staring now, not at the mirror, but to an area slightly thereunder, the following is what he viewed.

A locket, about five by five inches square, hung dingle-dangle at the end of a string. The latter, about five inches in length, was fastened to the rearview mirror's stem. Enclosed within said locket was a sight to behold. Let us observe it as the story unfolds hereinbelow.

The photograph of a naked-young woman showed her lying supine. Her vulva, which was exposed to the viewer, appeared enhanced because of the spread-eagle position of her legs. V-shaped and hairy, her genitalia likened to a beaver pelt, one that seemed to be bulging between two luscious limbs of smooth and tender flesh. A fissure, formed by the labia, was only plausibly visible. This was due to the pubic hairs, a crop of kinky ringlets that crawled over that opening. The clitoris, located about a third of the way down said fissure, issued therefrom like a clam's neck issues from the crack in its conch, when it attempts to snatch some kelp. Below the clitoris, in an area between it and the anus, a large-rubber penis remained firmly planted. Sandwiched in the vagina, it was suggestive of repeatedly penetrating that organ's wall. Such movement, the driver imagined, occurred at the will of the wench and her able right hand. The latter, reaching from under the right buttock, gripped the object and manipulated it. So vehement seemed the thrust that was generated by that appendage, one could say it resembled the systematic thrust of strokes by an oil pump's arm. Finally, judging by the quantity of vaginal mucus on the rubber contraption, it was evident that the shrew was engaging in the activity with very much gusto and no little gratification.

The driver reached for the locket with his right hand. While holding it still, he leaned forward, and, sticking out his tongue, he licked the area on the photo which displayed the wanton woman's vulva. At that instant, he felt blood rush to his penis. The latter behaved like a serpent, which, awakened or aroused from a temporary nap, swells and uncoils; then, it slithers in search of a victim to prick or a hole in which to slide and hide.

Concerning the appeasement of his concupiscent surge, the perverted *patron* thought it best to let the matter rest for the time being, even though his penis ached for a release. Perhaps he was dissuaded from masturbation by the thought of having to explain the appearance of semen stains in the crotch area of his pants. Be that as it may, he contented himself with inserting his key into the ignition, an act that, in itself, was suggestive and symbolic of fornication. Thus, giving said key a clockwise twist, he thereby caused the engine to turn over and his genitalia to be turned on.

Energized by his concupiscence, the prurient *patron* apparently felt a need to release a bit of libidinal energy. So, covering the accelerator pedal with the wrangler boot on his right foot, the man put the pedal to the metal, so to speak. Then, by pumping that device repeatedly, he revved the engine and thereby caused it to roar like race cars roar at the start of a heat.

Exhaust, meanwhile, as black and powdery as soot from a chimney, issued from a pipe at the truck's rear and clouded the immediate surroundings. The crewmembers, well within range of the toxic nebula, coughed and gasped while breathing its fumes. The driver remained unaffected by the pollution, since he was insulated from it by the closed cab in which he sat.

A smile, one of perverse satisfaction, cracked on the cold-fisted man's face, as he now focused on the vehicle's dash. Zeroing in on the tachometer, he watched its needle jump from one side of the dial to the other. He appeared fascinated while watching said needle waver with an astonishing volatility. Delighted, he was, upon seeing it flicker and flutter commensurately with his repeated activation of the throttle.

Stepping on the clutch pedal with the boot on his left foot, the exhilarated boss engaged that device. Next, he grabbed the gear stick with his right hand and jammed it into reverse. Then, he revved the engine again and again before popping the clutch and causing the rear wheels to spin. Wanting of traction, the wheels currently whirred as they spun in the pulverous desert soil. Then, after kicking up the topsoil, the tire treads eventually bit into the subsoil. Grounded, the vehicle moved. Backwards it jerked and leaped like a bucking bronco in a rodeo leaps! After jerking and leaping in the foregoing manner, the pickup truck proceeded to race in reverse! The backwards leap caused all twelve men to go crashing against the backside of the truck's cab! After the leap, each one of them scrambled to regain balance.

Meanwhile, the buzzards on high had been hovering over the scene hitherto described. Disturbed by the disorder and the ruckus below them, they had grown agitated. Wary, they were, and therefore, they winced somewhat upon seeing the pickup truck buck and subsequently race backwards. However, notwithstanding the disturbance and the din, those attentive fowl stayed focused on what they observed on land.

After racing in reverse for about thirty yards, the truck suddenly braked and skidded! Then, its front end spun clockwise for about ninety degrees before the vehicle came to a halt! Having occurred at the command of the infamous driver's foot and hands, the foregoing maneuvers reconfirmed his capacity for recklessness.

As a result of the most recent movement, the jostled bunch of crew members collided with the panel of the pickup truck's right side! Discombobulated once again, they struggled to reposition themselves.

By swerving and halting in the manner indicated above, the vehicle's shell ended up perpendicular to the canal. With its rear wheels just inches away from the waterway's bank, the truck remained at the brink of the drink, as some individuals might say. The vehicle's front end, meanwhile, was pointed at the junction where the two roads converged. We can remember that junction as being the one on which the truck had traveled while crossing the makeshift bridge that spanned the irrigation ditch. We'll also recall how the vehicle subsequently swerved to its right and nearly rolled over into the canal.

The vultures, still looming on high, then zeroed in on the stationery truck's bed. In particular, they observed the brood of twelve *campesinos,* whose torsos had been tossed about during the recent debacle.

Viewed from above, the jumbled bunch of peasants were a sight to behold. As a result of having lost balance, all of them had become disoriented. Hence, they began to wallow about while struggling to find their individual spots where they had originally sat. Similar to a herd of seals, ones that sometimes slip and slide on a slick rock's top, the wallowing farm workers slipped and slid on the mobile truck's bed.

The driver then stuck his head out the opened window on his side of the cab. While glancing over his left shoulder and back toward his shaken crew, he yelled out: "Hang on, *moochahchoes!* Ahm gonna give ya all a Mexican massage! Ha, ha, ha!"

While keeping the clutch pedal to the pickup truck's floor, the mad man applied the accelerator pedal not just once but many times more! Soon, he jammed the gear stick into first gear! Then, while revving the engine, he popped the clutch, as he had done before! The rear wheels then spun. Freely, they whirred until their treads grabbed solid soil, which caused the vehicle to advance.

Lunging forward, the pickup truck likened to a horse, one that is in the act of hurdling a hedge or jumping the fence of a barnyard's corral! As the shell lunged forward, the group of crewmembers went crashing into the tailgate! Then, as the truck raced forward, all of them again found themselves struggling to regain position! Indeed, they continued to wallow about on the pickup truck's bed as they had done previously. Thoroughly discombobulated, again, their bodies likened, to swine, this time! Yes, to swine they bore a semblance, the kind that wade and wallow in waste or swill! As the men wallowed, moreover, they also groped, and by groping, they grabbed whatever or whomever they could seize in an attempt to regain and maintain their equilibrium!

How fortunate it was that the tailgate had remained shut at the moment when the shell leaped forward. Had that not been the case, the jostled bunch of farmhands would have slid off from the vehicle's bed like rubbish from a dump truck, and they would have subsequently fallen into the swift waters of the deeply dug canal.

The pickup truck then darted toward the aforementioned junction of the two roads. Upon arriving there, it proceeded to cross the makeshift bridge that spanned the ditch and to subsequently advance along the same road it had traveled earlier that morning upon its arrival at the scene. Bucking, then bouncing, the vehicle also bounded on the boreen's uneven surface like a horse-drawn buckboard would be inclined to do! Indeed, the latter is sometimes seen to buck, bounce, and bound when drawn over potholes on back country roads.

As a result of the foregoing activity, the crew members on the truck's bed bobbed! Yes, bob and bounce they did, synchronously with the vehicle's unrelenting volatility! What a discomfort that must have been to that crew of twelve daunted men! Even the driver bounced about while remaining seated in the cab. However, his discomfort was significantly mitigated by the springs in the cab's seat, which tended to cushion the ride.

The only aggravation the *patron* was experiencing was the annoyance that emanated from his erection, one which had been nagging at him for some time. Presently prodded by the truck's jerking movements, said erection refused to subside. Unrelenting, indeed, was its demand for the placation of an insatiable urge. Most males who have passed puberty can relate to the driver's current vexation.

In the sky, a few of the looming buzzards separated themselves from the rest of the group. Lagging behind, they began to descend. In corkscrew swirls, they gravitated to the site where the body parts of the dead dog lay, in addition to bodies of wounded birds. The latter, by then, had surely expired. The foregoing vultures were bound to feed on whatever they could acquire.

Meanwhile, the remaining buzzards on high continued to monitor the mobile machine as it advanced along the dirt road. Viewed from above, the truck bore a semblance to a motorboat. Colored red, it very visibly evinced itself. Bobbing and weaving while edging along the road's bumpy surface, the vehicle appeared to be bucking a tidal flow in the troubled waters of a treacherous sea!

The crew of twelve, still bouncing about on the pickup truck's bed, used both hands to hold their sombreros in place. Struggling to grab their hats by the rim, they purported to secure them in place.

Intent, the men were, on shading their heads from the blinding rays of a mid-morning sun which, at that moment, was shining down on the vehicle at an angle of about forty-five degrees.

Sparkling on the truck's rearview mirrors, ones that sprouted on each side of its cab, said rays glimmered so that they dazzled the eyes of those who chanced to glance their way.

The free-floating vultures proved to be an exception to the hindrance mentioned above. Gliding, diving, then careening, they circled over, around, and above the vehicle. Floating thereabout in the foregoing manner, the volant fowl were able to avoid the directness of the mirrors' blinding radiance. As a result, they peered at the mirror on the driver's side; and, snatching furtive glances every now and then, they managed to monitor the man's activity, or lack thereof.

The boss' fat-porky face shone on the glassy surface of the mirror to his side of the cab. His eyes, staring blank, seemed to suggest that he wasn't focused on anything in particular. Most likely, he continued to be in the prurient trance that was prodded by his earlier view of that naughty-lewd nude!

So deep in thought was the perverted *patron* that he neglected to observe a person who was well within the path of his sights. At a distance of about twenty-five yards from the truck's front end, the individual was walking on the shoulder of the road's right side. Viewed from behind, the person appeared to be a young Mexican male of about medium size. Judging by his indumentum, one could readily say that he was of peasant stock. Who could he have been?

Before long, the pickup truck caught up with the preambulating peasant and proceeded to pass him. Dust, stirred by the truck's churning tires, rose from the road's surface. Clouding the ambience, it momentarily camouflaged the pedestrian particularly his bust and visage. Moments later, said dust settled, and the individual's face appeared in the mirror of the mobile machine's right side. Unmistakably, the face was that of the Mexican youth whom the driver had abrasively rejected back at the bank of the wide canal.

As the vehicle distanced itself from the ambulant boy, the crewmembers spotted him. Having recognized the lad, they seized the moment and decided to lend a helping hand. Thus, gesticulating and calling out *sottovoce,* several of them beckoned the boy to join the group.

"*¡Psst, psst! ¡Oye, joven! ¡Vente! ¡Arrímate!*

Trotting, the youth caught up with the truck and the twelve *campesinos.* Reaching the tailgate, he placed his hands thereupon. Next, he leapt toward it and attempted to climb onto the pickup truck's bed. Meanwhile, a couple of the *campesinos* knelt down near the inside portion of the tailgate. The two of them, one on each side of the boy, reached out and, grabbing him by the arms, pulled him over the tailgate and onto said bed.

The activity described hereinbefore resembled a rescue effort of a maritime kind. For example, let us imagine two seafaring men who are in the act of saving a sailor, one that has shipwrecked on the high seas. Reaching out from the gunnels of their lifeboat, the men attempt to grab the swimmer as he struggles to stay afloat. Tugging, they pull the sailor onto the deck of their craft.

After pulling the lad over the tailgate and onto the truck's bed, the two rescuers dragged him for about two or three feet and propped his torso up in a seated position between both of them. The other peasants, meanwhile, moved to one side in order to create space for the newcomer.

All thirteen of the *campesinos* were seated in the characteristic *pow-wow* posture. Positioned close to one another, they concurrently and synchronously endured the bumps from the humps and the potholes as well! Moreover, with their backs to the bow and eyes to the stern, so to speak, they faced the glare from the mid-morning sun, as the vehicle proceeded to venture westward.

The road, like all of the ones thereabout, seemed endless. Flanked by two irrigation ditches, one on each side, it continued for about twenty miles directly to the vast valley's center where it merged with the aforementioned highway that ran from north to south. Continuous, the foregoing road's trajectory cut through the jungle of verdure uninterrupted except for an intersection every seven or eight hundred yards.

Monotonous was the journey for the ferried farmhands. Tedious as well, it prompted them to seek relief. Therefore, each one of them bent his legs and drew his knees up to the chest area. Then, embracing the legs with both arms, they each used the kneecaps to cushion the head.

The crouched *campesinos* looked up from time to time in order to examine the surroundings. Those who were seated near the truck's rear peered downward and saw the road's crest of grass for a crown, one that separated two rugged tire tracks. Notwithstanding the intensity with which the men gazed, the view was ephemeral, since tracks and crown constantly evanesced in clouds of dust that were formed by the truck's turning treads.

Glancing to their left every now and then, and looking to the right as well, the perusing peasants viewed crops of tassel-tipped stalks. Towering and ubiquitous, each of the crops tended to daunt the viewer like a tidal wave might daunt any bystander or bather as its gathering mass swells and prepares to crash on an ocean's shore.

While the peasants yielded to an overwhelming discomfort, that which was caused by the roughness of the ride, the man at the helm proceeded to pilot them westward. Keeping both hands wrapped around the steering wheel's upper portion, he gripped tightly and thereby managed to maintain the stated direction of the vehicle's course.

As he drove, the man's eyes proceeded to stare straight ahead for the majority of the time. However, every now and then he snatched furtive glances at the pleasure-seeking shrew in the photo. This, we can recall, hung dingle-dangle from the cab's rearview mirror. Strung in the manner and spot described above, the lusty lady's image danced synchronously with every bump of the vehicle's volatile shell. Wickedly erotic were the lewd nude's jiggling motions! So explicitly demonstrative was the lascivious act in which she was engaged, that she excited the libidinous *patron* beyond measure!

Aroused, thus, the gaping man now perused the vamp's vulva. Viewing it intensely, he saw a V-shaped hump with a clump of kinky, dark hairs. Shiny black, like the shell of a scorpion's body, the crawly hairs contrasted sharply with the wench's white skin. Crawling over said hump, moreover, the crop of ringlets tended to camouflage the vulva's vertical crevice. We can recall that much of the above is a depiction of what we observed earlier in the story. The following is a more current episode of the similar topic.

The lusting man now conjured up a lifelike scene. For example, he imagined the power of the woman's vaginal muscles completely dominating the penis. Expanding and contracting involuntarily, they appeared to be drawing it into a succulent vortex of raw, liver-like flesh! Engulfed and devoured by the foregoing vortex, the penis momentarily dropped out of view! Then, ejected, it subsequently reappeared! Yes, disappearing, then reappearing repeatedly, it called to mind the motility of an oil pump's greasy shank!

Overwhelmed by concupiscence, the gaping voyeur eventually surrendered to the temptation. Thus, while keeping his left hand on the steering wheel, he used the right to unzip the fly on his trousers. Next, using that same hand, he massaged the crotch area for a moment or so before taking hold of a soon-to-be bony erection. Gripping the latter, he yanked it out and exposed its shank-like form to the bright light of day. Behold a fully erected penis! Measuring about eight inches in length, it pointed upward and out like a gun that was mounted on the bow of a warship.

Clenching his erection, the perverted man began to slide its epidermis to and fro. Stroking himself so, he repeatedly covered and uncovered the foreskin, which was a crimson-colored flap of flesh that capped the organ's protruding tip. *Pant* the *patron* soon did, in the manner in which a dehydrated mastiff pants in the heat of a torrid summer day! While the man panted, he also grunted! At the climactic moment, moreover, he even emitted groans! Ejaculating, then, his penis spat spurts of spittle-like sperm which splattered the instrument panel of the vehicle's dash!

The depraved man's pleasure was ephemeral. Being transitory, it left much to be desired in terms of sexual gratification. Yes, appeased, but teased, he eagerly longed for more excitement.

After discharging its fluid, the erection immediately softened. Limp, it now bore a semblance to a deflated balloon, the kind that is sausage-like in shape. Lifeless, thus, the organ was easily stuffed back into the crotch of the man's pants.

Subsequently, the driver reached into the right pocket of his trousers and extracted a handkerchief. Employing the latter as a cloth, he used it to fastidiously wipe the semen stains from the instrument panel on the vehicle's dash.

Having grown self-conscious about whether or not the crewmembers had witnessed his lewd behavior, the *patron* swung around to his right, and, glancing furtively through the window at the cab's rear, he eyeballed each man in the back. Totally focused on that which was occupying his mind at the time, the driver failed to notice that the newcomer had joined the group of peasants and was presently seated amongst the twelve of them. While the boss glanced at the group of peasants, he noticed that all continued to sit in *pow-wow* position with their backs to the truck's cab. He also observed that each one seemed oblivious to everything save an indefatigable capacity for enduring a hot desert sun and an uncomfortable ride.

Reassured that his act of masturbation had gone unobserved, the driver turned back around. Confident and relieved as a result of his inspection, he faced straight ahead and focused on the portion of the road to be traveled.

Gazing forward and slightly to his left, the perverted *patron* spotted a jackrabbit, which, having leapt out in front of the truck's bumper, was attempting to hop across the road. Startled, the impulsive man instinctively swung the steering wheel clockwise and attempted to run the creature over before it reached the other side of the road. However, the vehicle was no match for the elusive hare, whose pursuer nearly drove his truck off the right shoulder while chasing it thither. Whence there sprung another jackrabbit which caused the driver to turn the wheel counterclockwise in order to make contact with it. But, just as has been previously noted, the truck was not quick enough for the prancing hare. The latter dashed across the road and leaped over the irrigation ditch, then it vanished in the jungle of stalks.

The foregoing activity repeated itself over and over during a good part of the journey. It was as if all the rabbits in those surroundings had conspired to taunt the sadistic driver by deceptively leading him from one side of the road to the other. Meanwhile, the vehicle proceeded to zig-zag and swerve like a lifeboat that was bucking an unyielding tide!

Intent upon killing the creatures, the reckless boss continued to aim his truck at them as they crossed from shoulder to shoulder in the manner described above. Then, all of a sudden, something caught his attention. Straight ahead, at a distance of about three hundred yards, there was a certain activity. Movement, one of machinery and of individuals, had entered the path of the driver's sights and was preventing him from seeing beyond it.

Having once identified the foregoing activity, the man at the helm immediately stopped chasing jackrabbits and headed directly toward that which was familiar to him.

Moments later, truck driver and crew arrived at a large clearing of white sand. Measuring about the size of a football field, it occupied the westernmost portion of the plot through which we have seen the individuals travel. Trailer bins, large and colored yellow, occupied much of the sandy clearing. Some were filled to the brim with full-bodied ears of corn. They were to be towed, via the highway mentioned at the beginning of our story, to a nearby packing shed in the southern part of the valley. Other bins were empty. At that time, they were being hitched to tractors and would soon be towed through unharvested fields of corn. Each empty bin would be accompanied by twelve pickers and a driver.

In the meantime, the young *Lazarillo,* who had stealthily joined the group at an earlier point in time, seized the opportunity to slip away from said group without being observed. That is to say, having noticed that the *patron* was distracted by the commotion at the site, he secretly climbed over the truck's tailgate and jumped onto the road's crown. Next, after darting to the right shoulder, he leapt over the irrigation ditch, and, similar to one of the aforementioned jackrabbits, he quickly vanished in the towering maze of verdure. Hiding there, in a spot that was not far from the aforementioned commotion, he waited and listened.

The prurient *patron* then yelled to a supervisor, who was dispatching crews of pickers to the empty bins. "Hey, Clem! Can ya use a fresh crew a greasers? They're all oiled up and ready to go! Why, they was a humpin' their ole ladies when I come by for em!"

"Hell, yes! Bring 'em here! Greasers are greasers, I always say." Replied the supervisor. Then, he added: 'Tell me, Zeke, ya still fuckin' that spicky chicky in Indio?"

"You'd better believe it! When I ain't fuckin' her, I'm a doin' the Mrs! Get the picture?" Answered the truck driver.

"Ah hear ya loud and clear! Ain't nothin' like a steady piece a ass to keep a man fit!"

From his hiding spot in the forest of stalks, *Lazarillo* watched Zeke drive his truck from the road along which he had led his crew. He saw him advance onto the sandy clearing for about twenty-five yards. He then watched him turn right at about ninety degrees and proceed in the direction of an empty bin.

Zeke was reckless, as we have noted. Hence, while he headed toward the aforementioned bin, he accelerated. And when he got to within five yards of it, he slammed on the brakes and nearly rammed the bin broadside! As soon as the truck came to a complete stop, Clem approached the tailgate to unlatch it. After jerking the chain that served to keep the gate from lowering, he motioned to the crew to get out and to line up alongside the foregoing bin. While eyeballing each one of them carefully, he uttered some obscenities.

"*¡Ahreeba, ahreeba, cheengones!¡ No Cheengahr!¡ Ah trabahahr - ah trahbhahar!*"

Obediently, the twelve pickers got out of the truck, and, following instructions, they lined up along side the bin. Eventually, they were ordered to climb onto the empty bin's bed. There, they waited for a tractor driver who would transport them to harvest a nearby crop.

In the meantime, Zeke drove off to round up more pickers, and *Lazarillo,* seizing the opportunity of the truck driver's absence, decided to try his luck on Clem, the supervisor.

The Mexican lad surreptitiously slipped out from his cover and walked right up to Clem. The latter was standing with his back to the bin, which he had recently loaded with the crew of twelve. *Lazarillo* introduced himself and asked Clem if he could join one of the crews. The following was the man's response: "Ya gotta be shitin' me! Why, just by lookin' atcha I cain't tell if yur a pussy or a boy whose balls ain't dropped yet! Get lost and don't bother me! This is man's work!"

After uttering his last sentence, Clem shoved the boy aside and walked away to fetch a tractor driver for his recently assembled crew. A moment later, one of the crewmembers in the bin called out to the boy *sottovoce:* "*¡Psst, psst, joven!¿Por qué no vas preguntando allá?¡Dicen que hay trabajo!*"

By his language and gesture, the crewmember was suggesting that *Lazarillo* inquire about work in the packing shed to the south. Tearful but hopeful, the youngster thanked the worker. Then, he crossed the sandy clearing and headed for the highway in order to hitch a ride south.

The sun hung directly overhead now, and the temperature reached well into the hundreds. A haze, caused by dust, exhaust, and insecticides, hovered over an unending carpet of tassel-tipped stalks. The obfuscation thickened as a result of the growing heat and a complete absence of wind. Before long, the entire valley would resemble a colossal dustbowl contained by two *cordilleras,* the one on the east and the other on the west.

An effluvium emanated from dumps of dung and puddles of urine. Deposited randomly in furrows by beast and by man, the waste cooked and broiled in the summer heat. At the same time, a rancid miasma issued from rotting carcasses; and, by commingling with the foregoing effluvium, it generated an offensive stench, one that likened to that of portable toilets. Therein, feces, urine, and menstrual discharges are inadequately treated by applying excessive amounts of ammonia.

Lazarillo walked along the road's right shoulder, holding his head down and tilted slightly forward. He looked up from time to time; and, glancing straight ahead, he saw blurry-vaporous heat waves rise wiggly-waggly from the highway's asphalt surface. At the same time, he listened attentively and attempted to hear whether or not any vehicles were coming his way. Whenever that occurred, he would turn around to face the approaching vehicle and would hold out his right hand in a thumb up position. Most of the vehicles were pickup trucks whose drivers were towing loaded bins of corn to the packing shed in the south. Said drivers seemed indifferent to the young hitchhiker. The majority didn't even bother to acknowledge his presence.

The more he distanced himself from the aforementioned clearing of sand, the more alone *Lazarillo* felt. His sense of solitude grew even more intense as he penetrated a seemingly uninhabited wilderness of tall, leafy stalks. For him, the feeling was one of apprehension, the kind that an explorer experiences when he is entering uncharted land. Yes, solitary and uneasy the peasant boy remained until...

A whirring sound, the pitch of which resembled that of a mosquito, pierced the lad's left eardrum. The noise grew gradually and prompted him to look upward and to the left at about ten o'clock. A helicopter, approaching from the east at an altitude of about some two hundred feet, was beginning to descend and head directly toward the youngster. Its whirring sound grew louder as the craft drew nigh to where the boy stood. Moreover, its overhead propeller spun rapidly and thereby emitted a heavy pounding noise, the kind that is associated with a chopper.

Terrified, the Mexican lad instinctively dropped face down to the ground similar to a soldier ducking to avoid fire. Next, he covered the backside of his head with both hands. His *sombrero,* caught in a whirlwind that was created by the craft, blew away like tumbleweed in a gusty desert wind. Meanwhile, chopper and pilot passed about fifteen feet above the boy's strewn body and began to fly over the nearby crop of stalks.

Swiftly westward the chopper flew. While gliding above the carpet of tassels as if it were going to mow them, it left a grayish-white trail of pesticides behind. At the same time, the chopper's propeller generated hurricane-force winds that caused the stalks to bend in the manner in which bamboo tends to bend when lashed by the gale of a tropical storm.

After proceeding for a couple of miles, the helicopter soared. Then, likening to a dragonfly, it hovered in thin air for a few seconds. Next, it careened to its port side and made about a hundred-and-forty-degree turn before descending and heading back in the direction of the highway. While combing the carpet of tassels again, the chopper left another trail of dust.

Lazarillo, in the meantime, had risen to his feet. Having thought that the helicopter was going to continue westward, he fetched his *sombrero* and resumed his journey. However, upon seeing the aircraft return, he quickly leapt over the irrigation ditch that paralleled the highway and dashed for cover in the jungle of stalks.

When the chopper got back to the highway, it soared and hovered above it. Then, after its pilot plotted a new course, the craft repeated the process described above and dusted a new patch of stalks. Once he combed an area of some five or six square miles, said pilot left in search of another crop to dust.

The Mexican youth listened for the whirring sound to grow faint and die. Then, assured that it was safe for him to expose himself, he left his cover, returned to the highway, and got back to his task.

Solar rays of the early noon hour were so intense that they melted the highway's asphalt. This likened to molten pitch, the kind that is used on roofs. Spongy and pliable, the melting substance yielded to the steps taken by the Mexican boy as he proceeded to walk southward.

Said solar rays singed stalks as well. Tassels, once of a hearty amber coloration, had become a bleached yellow. Leaves of the stalks, formerly green and blade-like in shape, were parched and shriveled. Ears, previously erect and fleshy, were beginning to droop commensurately with the lifeless stalks from which they sprouted. Excrements and rotting carcasses, cooking in the afternoon's calidity, pervaded and polluted the air. Offensive, the fetor plagued the senses of anyone present.

As he walked, the young peasant grew weary. Afflicted by the elements described above, he felt nauseous and somewhat feverish. Difficult moments such as the one which *Lazarillo* was experiencing at that time were ones in which he conjured, in his imagination, the images and voices of his deceased father and his older brother. Exhortative and admonitory was their advice. For example, let us observe the following:

"¡Sig' adelante, m'hijo! ¡No te desespereh! ¡Que Dios t'ayude!"

"¡Andale, manito!¡Escúchale a papá! ¡Y sig' adelante!¡Que Dios te bendiga!"

The voices were telling the youth to keep forging ahead. They even invoked God's intervention. Let us continue to observe how emphatic the lad's father became:

"¡Yo t'ayudareh desde aquí con mis oraciones, pero tú tieneh que luchar, hijito! ¡La vida eh bien dura! ¡Mucho depende de ti! ¡Tu mamá y tus hermanos te necesitan! ¡ Sin ti, nuhay esperanza!"

Insistent upon making his point, the man stressed the importance of *Lazarillo's* dedicating himself to the survival of the family. There were times when the lad even pictured his father and older brother dialoguing between themselves about his particular situation. The following is an example:

"*¡No te preocupeh, papá! Estoh seguro que too saldrá bieng. ¡N'olvideh que Lázaro eh hijo tuyo, y que por eso, tieneh um par de güevos bieng grandeh!*"

"*¡Ya lo creo! ¡Pero eh tan joven!.. ¡Pos, espero que too saldrá bieng como tú dices!... ¡Quizáh con la ayuda de El!*"

Moments, instants, and sometimes hours found the boy abandoned to his phantasmagorical folly which is depicted herein.

Oblivious to anything save the voices and images of his trance, the Mexican youth hadn't, at first, noticed an automobile which, having approached him from the rear, slowed down and came to a stop about twenty yards ahead of him.

Beep, beep! "Wanna ride, baby?" Asked a female motorist who was seated behind the steering wheel.

The sound of the vehicle's horn, in addition to the driver's voice, awakened *Lazarillo* from his cataleptic state. Stupefied, he first came to a halt, then he gingerly proceeded to walk toward the car. This was a flashy, red-colored convertible. Of a recent model, its bumpers of chrome and glassy rearview mirrors sparkled in the early noon glow.

"C'mon, sugar! Hop in! I won't bite cha! Ha, ha!" The driver added.

The Mexican youth looked and saw an attractive blonde, who, keeping her left hand on the steering wheel and her right arm extended over the seat's backrest, greeted the boy again and invited him to enter. While gazing at the lad over her right shoulder, she insisted: "Hurry up, sweetie! I ain't got all day!"

A tune, one of a popular repertoire, blared from the car's radio: "**Pretty woman, walking down the street, pretty woman, the kind you wanna meet, pretty woman...!**"

Lazarillo stared at the motorist. She was a sexy woman in her twenties, whose shoulder-length hair appeared disheveled by the wind. She wore sunglasses, the darkness of which contrasted with her skin of a eucharistic whiteness and her hair of a moonlight hue. A blouse of a pastel pink loosely covered her torso. The latter was slender and firm. Unbuttoned about a third of the way down, the woman's blouse formed a V-shape in the front. This opening exposed an enticing cleavage and a pair of bulging bosoms.

The lass's lips were fleshy. Crimson-colored, they resembled two strips of raw liver. Moist and somewhat wry, they conveyed a suggestive wantonness to the gaping, young voyeur.

Gasping, as he gaped, the young male grew nervous and perturbed while viewing the vamp who continued to summon him from the vehicle. The current event was invasively visceral for the youngster. It was one that resulted in an accelerated heart rate and a libidinal anxiety, one that pervaded his entire being and begged for a complete placation. Soon thereafter, the young male began to undergo the masculine discomfort that occurs when becoming sexually aroused while standing. Self-conscious, he felt, when his erected penis visibly bulged in the crotch of his pants. We should note that *Lazarillo* was a virgin whose sexual activities were limited to masturbation and nocturnal emissions. Thus, he was prone to become readily excited by sexual thoughts and encounters. By contrast, the foxy motorist was apparently accustomed to intimate contact with males. Hence, her aggressiveness proved both inhibiting and arousing to the youth.

Caught in a quandary, the youth felt bewildered. The woman was voluptuous and astonishingly gorgeous, he thought. However, what troubled him was how he would conduct himself while in her presence. What would he do with her? He asked himself. How would she react upon discovering that he was not experienced in sexual matters? What if he were to ejaculate prematurely? The foregoing thoughts were ones that rushed through the lad's brain while the vamp stared at him.

As the boy drew gingerly nigh to the automobile, the woman got a closer look at him. Gazing at the solitary figure, she noticed how pathetic was his appearance. Yes, there he stood just feet away from her. He measured about five feet-four inches tall and was as skinny as a rail. Moreover, dressed in soiled- tattered clothes, and capped by a misshapen *sombrero,* the peasant resembled a tatterdemadalion.

Having previously observed him from afar, the woman had not gotten a clear idea of *Lazarillo's* impoverished condition. Now, watching him reach for the passenger door's handle, she managed to get a better look at him. Using her right hand to remove the sunglasses, she subsequently proceeded to inspect the youth who was attempting to enter her vehicle. Upon scrutinizing him, the wanton wench immediately put her glasses back on. Next, she placed the engine in low gear, stepped on the accelerator, and left the poor young peasant in the dust.

As she drove off, the vamp's blonde hair blew in the breeze like the strands of a cheerleader's pom-pom swish frantically through the air during an athletic contest. In the meantime, another popular tune blared from the car radio: *"You've lost that lovin 'feelin, oh-oh that lovin feelin'! You 've lost that lovin 'feelin' now it's gone, gone, gone, oh-oh-oh-oh-oh!"*

As he watched the wench drive away, the young Mexican exhibited a look of bewilderment. On the one hand, he undoubtedly felt rejected by her. On the other, he probably experienced a certain relief at not having to prove himself sexually. Be that as it may, the lonely lad resumed his pace, walking along the highway's right shoulder.

Within a moment or so, the voice and image of his father reappeared in *Lazarillo's* imagination. Emphatically, he warned his son to beware of wayward women:

"¡No pierdas tiempo pensando en mujeres como ésa, chico! ¡Ella no fue más que una puta!¡Ese tipo de mujer no te trae sino problemas!"

The sun's rays now singed the boy's right flank, as he longingly watched the automobile disappear in the heat waves that were rising wiggly-waggly from the road's asphalt surface. At the same time, he listened to the voices of his father and his older brother who were continuing to admonish him.

Eventually, the early noon's heat created an insufferable dryness, one that awakened the lad from his reverie. Instinctively, he then turned to his right and began to walk in the direction of the irrigation ditch. Wearily, he staggered there. Kneeling down at its bank, he used both of his hands to scoop up generous portions of murky water; and, drawing it to his mouth, he thereby sought to quench an almost insatiable thirst. However, not satisfied with the amounts of liquid he was scooping with his hands, the youngster removed his *sombrero,* and, submerging his entire head in the stream, he gulped water to his heart's content!

Sky-high, meanwhile, a flock of five vultures hovered. Soaring, floating, careening, then gliding, they sailed through the air like kites in wind currents of a balmy spring day. While floating there above, they peered downward and kept the peasant boy in their sights.

Having replenished his feverish body with water from the ditch, *Lazarillo* returned to the road's shoulder and persevered in his journey southward. From time to time, he would raise his head and glance at the road to be traveled. The heat waves, still rising from the highway's surface, tended to blur the boy's vision. Tar, meanwhile, melting and sticking to his *huaraches,* slowed his pace considerably.

Approaching the peasant from the opposite direction came a diesel truck traveling at full speed. While passing him, the driver sounded the horn and waved. That was the friendliest gesture anyone had bestowed on him all day, thought the boy while looking up and waving back at the driver. Then, as he prepared to drop his head down again, his eyes caught a glimpse of something.

Straight ahead of the lad, and slightly to the right, a large piece of sheet metal sparkled in the solar glare about a half of a mile away.

Blinding, it dazzled *Lazarillo*. Let us get an airborne perspective of what the boy's eyes had discovered.

Viewed by the hovering vultures, a roof shimmered like a large beacon. Located in the middle of a spacious sandy clearing, moreover, roof and clearing together were surrounded by an ocean of tassel-capped stalks. The high-spying buzzards studied that which had just come into their view. The following is what they saw:

The aforementioned roof slanted in the shape of a modified A-frame. Lengthwise, it ran from east to west and covered an area of about seventy yards. Made of tin-plated steel, it beamed in the sunlight, as we have noted. Widthwise, said roof probably measured about forty to fifty yards; and, from the ground to its highest point, approximately thirty-five yards.

As the buoyant birds got closer to what they were observing, they noticed that the roof was sustained by a rectangular frame of steel beams. These, together with the roof, created an enclosure. A packing shed, as it is called in agricultural vocabulary, provided the workers and the produce with protection from the torrid sun's rays. Moreover, open on all four sides, it allowed good air circulation during times of operation. Above the roof top, running lengthwise at its apex, was a sign that read SUNRISE PRODUCE COMPANY, INC.

Near the shed's east end was a one-story building made of bricks. Much smaller than the shed, it probably contained no more than two or three separate rooms. On the front door, which faced north, was a sign with the word: *OFFICE.*

Shed and office together occupied over an acre of the aforementioned clearing of sand. The latter was about the size of three football fields. On the south side of the shed, railroad tracks ran alongside the building. On the north side, about seventy yards from said shed, was a large pavilion of a sort. Thereunder, bins full of fresh ears of corn were parked. Eventually, the produce would be processed.

The buzzards, still looming overhead, watched *Lazarillo* arrive at the foregoing clearing. Peering, they saw him hop across the irrigation ditch and trudge along through dirt and sand on his way toward the shed. Viewing him from their altitude was like watching a beetle crawl on a sandy beach.

Having reached the aforementioned pavilion, the Mexican boy paused for a moment to ask a shed hand for the foreman. The worker, a Mexican man who was hitching up a trailer to his tractor, pointed in the direction of the office. *Lazarillo* thanked the man and then followed his directions.

Upon approaching the office, the youth was distracted by noises from machinery and human activity that emanated from the shed's interior. Curious, he turned to his right and walked in the direction of the hullabaloo. Pausing, he observed the full-scale operation of the packing shed. Ears of corn, ones that had been recently harvested, were being visibly dumped from a bin onto a conveyor belt. This activity was facilitated by mechanically hoisting one side of the bin, and thereby allowing the produce to slide off the other side and onto said belt. It was then conveyed to a crew of graders. Standing alongside the belt, Mexican women graded the ears by separating the good ones from the ones that were worm infested. After that process, the good ears were transported, via another conveyor belt, to a tank of water. Ridded of insecticides by a good soaking in the tank, the produce was subsequently conveyed to other women who, lined up alongside another conveyor belt, received and packed the ears in five-dozen count crates. From there, the filled crates were transferred, via another conveyor belt, to box cars and diesel trailers where they were hand loaded by young Mexican men for distribution throughout various points of the United States.

Lazarillo was impressed by the foregoing movement and activity especially the very manly process of loading. Therefore, he turned around and eagerly headed for the office to inquire about employment. Having arrived there, the youngster knocked on the

door a couple of times and waited. After a few seconds, he heard
a female's voice instruct him to enter. Turning the knob slowly, he
opened the door and entered. Sheepishly, he removed his *sombrero;*
and, holding it with both hands at waist level, he tarried a tad or
two while staring straight ahead and downward at an area not far
from where he stood.

A young female receptionist, seated at a desk that faced the
entrance to the office, was typing frantically. Completely consumed
by the task at hand, her eyes did not stray from the typewriter.
Indeed, oblivious to all else, she didn't even bother to acknowledge
Lazarillo's presence when he first entered the room.

The newcomer timidly approached the receptionist's desk.
Continuing to hold his hat at waist level, he appeared humble and
obsequious. Meanwhile, he kept his eyes focused on the woman.
While staring at her, he could not help but admire her beauty. Hair,
reddish and arranged in a pony tail, was shoulder length. Neck and
shoulders were bare and cluttered with specks of many freckles.
Straps, the *spaghetti* type, sustained a cotton dress which was
colored a powder blue. Bosoms, blessed by a supple juvenescence,
blossomed on both sides of an inviting cleavage. Said bosoms and
cleavage beckoned the peasant boy's attention beyond measure.
Enchanted by her charm, he was almost speechless when she
looked up and made eye contact with him.

"Well, what do you want"? Asked the woman very tersely. At
the same time, she gave him a quick once over with a pair of eyes
whose color matched that of her dress.

In the meantime, a discrete scent of perfume had reached
the youngster's nostrils. Emanating from the woman's body, it
complemented her charm and proved to be as powerful as an
aphrodisiac. Discrete, as well, was the light shade of eye shadow
which called his attention. Lashes, too, were stunning. Curled, long
and black, the latter were in the shape of scorpions' tails.

Perusing the lass's beauty, the young peasant noticed that the
shape and contour of the rest of the woman's face were in perfect

proportion to her head and neck. Eyebrows, dark and pencil thin, appeared to be carefully sketched on a brow of alabaster white. Curving upward at the middle, especially when she glanced at something or someone, they evinced a certain superciliousness. Cheeks, moreover, rose colored and slightly plump, were separated by a delicate turned-up nose. Lips, sensuous and tainted ruby red, lacked only a smile. A chin, dimpled in the middle, in addition to two pixie-like ears, complemented her Creator's able work of art.

Compared to the lady's beauty, *Lazarillo's* appearance was deplorable. Sweaty and filthy from his journey, he resembled a crewmember who had just finished his shift. He was made aware of his repugnance as she frowned at him and asked, "Well, have you got a name?"

The youth gulped and then responded, "I am *Lazarillo del Cordero*. I am looking for work. May I please speak to the foreman?"

"Wait here." Ordered the receptionist.

Rising slowly from her chair, the woman turned to her left and walked to a closed door that was about fifteen feet from where she had been sitting. Carrying documents in her hand, she appeared very efficient and professional as she strutted across the office.

After knocking on the door, the lady waited for a few seconds until a gruff voice instructed her to enter. She did so and closed the door behind her. About five minutes passed before the receptionist reopened the door, exited the room and returned to her chair. Distracted by thoughts which probably had nothing to do with the young Mexican who was still standing in front of her desk, she seemed inattentive to him. After sitting down, she tidied up her desk a bit. Eventually, she looked up at the peasant boy and said, "Oh, yeah. Uh... he'll see you now."

Continuing to hold his hat at waist level, *Lazarillo* walked toward the foreman's office. After knocking, as the receptionist had done, the boy lingered there until he heard a cigar-charred voice growl, "C'mon in, Goddamit!"

Upon entering the room, the young peasant closed the door and peered straight ahead. Directly opposite him sat an individual at a desk. Face and bust were concealed by a newspaper which the man was supposedly reading. Smoke rings, in the shape of halos, rose from behind the newspaper. Legs and wrangler boots, extending forward on top of the desk, were massive like the hands that held the foregoing reading material. Buttocks and torso, big and round, concealed the seat and backrest which they occupied.

"Well, are ya gonna sit yur ass down or what?" Snarled the voice that came from behind the newspaper.

Lazarillo moved gingerly forward toward the area whencefrom came the voice, and slowly, he sat down in a chair that was directly in front of the foreman's desk.

There was a silence for about ten seconds. Then, the foreman discharged a fart. Rumbling from the seat of his pants, its fumes traveled right for the boy's face. Lucky for him the gas' stench was mitigated by the smell of cigar smoke.

Another ten seconds passed before the uncouth man whipped the newspaper together. Then, folding it in a rough and sloppy manner, he slapped it down on top of the desk, as if he was swatting a horsefly. Removing his legs from the desktop, he planted them thereunder. He stared at the lad, giving him the once-over. At the same time, the peasant got a good look at him.

Bald, except for a trim of hair on the cranium's backside and on the temples, the man's parietal bone shone in the light which entered a window behind him. Smooth and shiny, the man's head likened to that of a wax figure in a museum. Glasses, whose lens were as thick as coke bottle bottoms, remained fixed on the bridge of a potato-shaped nose. They magnified a pair of venomous eyes. These, beady and drab, revealed a certain spitefulness and a complete lack of luster. Nose, mouth, cheeks, and chin reminded one of the visage on a hog; ears were likened to those of a Brobdingnagian giant. Breasts, sagging within a khaki shirt, rested on his Buddha-like belly. Shoulders and arms resembled those of a grizzly.

Leaning forward, the fat man placed his elbows on the desktop. Meanwhile, puffing on his cigar, he inhaled a significant amount of smoke, which he subsequently blew in the peasant boy's face and caused him to exclaim, "What are you doing?"

"Quiet, *cholo!*" Retorted the foreman. Then, while keeping the cigar in his mouth, he smiled. Diabolic was his look, as he added: "Ahl ask the questions! Get the message, beaner? Fur starters, tell me yur name. Yuh got a name, doncha? Ah also wants to know what y'all wants here."

Lazarillo started to answer but before he was able to do so, the man interrupted, saying: "So ya wants a job, duz ya? How in da fuck can I hire you? Yur nuthin' but a piss ant! Why, ahl bet ya ain't even got hair on yur crotch!"

The young peasant grew angry at the man's crass remarks. Nevertheless, he repressed his indignation and asserted himself politely. "Please don't call me names." Then he added: "It is not necessary to be insulting."

"Insultin' huh? Well, how about spic?" Sneered the foreman.

"You already know why I am here. And please do not call me names." Wrangled the lad.

The dialogue then continued when the fat man said: "What's the matter, kid? Ashamed a yur heritage? Why, bein' a beaner ain't sa bad. Betterin bein' a nigger, that's fur goddam sure!"

"If you hate my people so much, why do you hire them to work for you?" Asked *Lazarillo.*

"Cuz you people is cheap labor. Besides, ahd never hire a white man to do a slave's job, anyways. And as far as niggers go, they're too fuckin' lazy."

While slumping back on his chair again, the foreman grabbed the newspaper, opened it, and resumed his reading. This time he refrained from putting his legs and feet on the desk.

A minute or so passed before the man whipped the newspaper together and then slapped it on the desk as he had done earlier. A mean look now beamed on his face as he said: "That's exactly what pisses me off! A *cholo* wantin' to be treated like a white man! You listen to me, Mex! When I say shit, you shit! When I say piss, you piss!"

Lazarillo was now filled with consternation. Indeed, feelings of rage and rancor pervaded his entire being, especially the entrails. Roused and almost spasmodic, he sought to regurgitate a vile-fetid bile which had inured to him from centuries of oppression. Adrenalin, a giant dosage of it, invasively charged his body. Full of aggression and out of control, the Mexican peasant was about to spit at the obese boss for being such an outrageous bigot. However, at that very moment, the man interjected, "So, yur lookin' fer work, huh?"

"Yes, sir!" Answered the boy eagerly.

At that instant, the image *of Lazarillo's* father and older brother reappeared in his imagination. Together with the images came a dialogue exchange by means of which the youngster was to receive encouragement and support. For example:

"*Bieng hecho, jijo. Sé güeno y humilde.*"

"*Eso es, manito. No te enojes. Al fin y al cabo, no valeh la pena... Hazle caso al patrón ... Le gusta esoh.*"

The foreman paused for a few seconds and then sat back in his chair and glanced aimlessly at the ceiling. Next, he sat up abruptly, and, while planting both elbows on the desk, he spoke to the peasant.

"Well, ya can see fur yurself that there ain't much business here. Why, take a good look fur yurself. In the shed, everybody is a standin' around playin' with his self. It don't look good, boy. Why, hell! Ahl probably have ta sell some a yur *compadres* down the river. In this business, that means sweatin' yur balls off a-pickin' corn with the greasy wetbacks. But, come back in a couple a days and ahl see if I can use ya."

Lazarillo diffidently got up from the chair, and, after thanking the foreman, he turned around and walked toward the door. Disappointed and confused the young peasant had become.

Recalling the voices of his father and older brother, he focused on what they had recently said to him and how it presented a contradiction to him. For example, they had told him to be obedient and humble, when at the same time, he remembered how indignant he felt when the foreman insulted him and how he felt like spitting at him. At that moment, he asked himself if it is wise to repress anger when it makes you unhappy to do so.

After leaving the man's office, the Mexican peasant directed a furtive glance at the receptionist who was completely absorbed in the task of typing. Preferring to exit the building unnoticed by her, he headed for the door without saying a word. He was upset and nervous. Hence, he preferred to avoid any condescending remarks she might make which would make him feel worse.

Immediately following the lad's departure, the foreman grasped the telephone on his desktop. While bringing the receiver to his right ear, he used the left index finger to dial a number that was as familiar to him as his Social Security. Two rings, then the other party answered: "Good afternoon. Sunrise Produce in San Francisco. Lucian speaking. How may I help you?"

"Hello, boss. Ya called this morning?" Asked the foreman. The following is the dialogue exchange that took place between the two parties:

"It's about time you returned my call! What are you guys running down there, a whore house, for Christ's sake?"

"Ahm real sorry, boss. We been busiern hell down here."

"Who in the hell is *we?* What do you think I've been doing all day, jacking myself off?"

"Sorry, sir. It won't happen again. Ah promise. Word of honor."

"Listen to me, you dressed up barrel of lard! I have several orders to fill for the East Coast and Chicago! Get all the help together and tell them to shake ass!"

"Ya can count on me. Ahl take care of it right away. Uh, by the way, boss. How much should we pay the hired help?"

"Same as always. Minimum wage! What in the fucking hell do you think we're running here, a homeless shelter?"

"No, sir. You is right, as usual. The problem is that many of the workers is threatnin' a strike. Some asshole named Chavez is organizing migrant workers in a lot of areas in California. It's just a matter a time, and we is gonna have ta meet the demands of the union."

"When are your balls gonna drop, Hank? You useless piece of white trash shit! I say fuck Chavez and fuck his union, too! If you don't have the balls to get things going the way I want them to go, you can pack your bags, your wife and kids, and your mistress and go back to living on the streets where I found you when you didn't have a pot to piss in or a window to throw it out of! Furthermore, you can tell those ugly greasers that they have one of two alternatives. They can keep their jobs and eat my shit, or they can go back to taking *siestas* under a Joshua tree! If they should refuse my offer, they'll be replaced by a shit load of gukes from South East Asia! Oh, and before I forget, I want quality merchandise to come out of my shed! I've been getting all kinds of complaints from the customers. The last few shipments of corn had worms so big that they were wearing sunglasses while basking in the heat of the box cars!"

"Absolutely, boss. No problem. Ahl get to it right away." Affirmed Hank.

"That's more like it. And remember, Hank, if you fuck things up for me, my foot's going to be so far up your ass you'll need a crowbar to get it out!" Snarled Lucian.

"No need to worry, sir. Everything is under control." Assured the foreman.

"You can bet your balls it will be!" Responded the boss.

As soon as Lucian finished his last sentence, there was an audible click, which was followed by a dial tone from the receiver. Such was the manner in which the man usually ended a telephone conversation, particularly when he was upset, which was most of the time.

On the very next day, the shed hands began working as diligently as they were accustomed to doing when certain conditions were favorable. Indeed, high temperatures, a general absence of insects, and an abundance of water, in addition to a large pool of diehard laborers, were variables that always promised an accelerated harvest.

In the fields, the crews of pickers worked around the clock. Each crew, three in all, would commit to an eight-hour shift. During the night hours, the pickers would labor under the beaming lights from a tractor.

In the meantime, *Lazarillo* returned to the office as the foreman had instructed him to do. Restrained and inhibited the lad felt, so much so that he winced when the man grumbled, "Yur back!"

"Yes, sir. I want to know if you are going to give me a job." Asserted *Lazarillo* as he sat down slowly in the chair opposite Hank. Then, they resumed their dialogue:

"Where did you work before, boy?"

"I picked citrus for Acme Produce on the west side of the valley."

"Well, what happened? How come ya ain't working thar no more?"

"I was only a part-time worker. They paid me cash by the day. The boss said he could not use me anymore because business was too slow. I have been looking for work for about three months."

"How much did they pay ya?"

"A dollar thirty an hour."

Hank paused for a while, during which time he glanced aimlessly at various indeterminate spots in the office. Meanwhile, he avoided eye contact with the youngster. Then, sitting on the edge of his seat, he leaned forward; and, looking at the Mexican boy in the eyes, he declared: "Well, we got enough help to fill our orders. Better look somewhere else for a job. Besides, yur too young, boy. Go back to mama. Ya got a mama, doncha? Nothin' doin' here. Scram! Vamoose! Go sniff yur kid sister's bicycle seat!"

Lazarillo got up slowly. Rejected and dejected, he remained standing for a moment or two. Drooping his head so that his chin touched the upper chest area he began to sob. As his eyes watered, he tried to hide the tears but did not succeed in doing so. Teardrops, two of them, ran down his cheeks and fell onto the office floor. Embarrassed, the youngster turned around and headed for the door.

The young Mexican left the office and began the long journey back home. After leaving the office building, he returned to the highway and walked north. While trudging along the road's shoulder, he held his head down; and, adjusting his *sombrero* so that it rested on the parietal bone of his skull, he protected the head and shoulders from the overhead beams of the scalding sun.

Oppressive, the early noon's calidity compounded the lad's feeling of hopelessness and drudgery. Moreover, overpowering was the fetor that emanated from the feces, urine, and decomposing cadavers, all of which occupied sundry areas of the corrugated ground. Insecticides, at the same time, covered tassels and leaves. Ethereal, their fetid scent rose commensurately with the heat waves that climbed wiggly-waggly from the crops' tasseled surfaces. Penetrant, their chemical venom entered the youth's eyes, nostrils, and throat, creating an acute state of asphyxia and dizziness.

In want of consolation, the Mexican peasant inserted his right hand in the pocket of his trousers and withdrew rosary beads. Winding them around his hand, he held them taut. Using the thumb and index finger, he squeezed the beads individually and recited a Hail Mary for each one.

While *Lazarillo* prayed, the images of his father and older brother reappeared in his brain. Habitual was the foregoing tendency, we know. Let us note, at the same time, that he had recently become cognizant that his predisposition to such a habit was misguided and misleading. First of all, the images and voices were phantasmal. Created by him in his imagination, they had no bearing on reality. In short, there was no way in which the boy could attain proper guidance by confiding in them. Second, their general message lacked sound judgment, as we have discovered. That is to say, there was a conflict between the advice he attained from the voices and his very own proclivities.

Aware of the delusion that resulted from his reverie, the Mexican lad prayed with unrelenting fervor to rid himself of his folly. Nevertheless, his efforts to dispense with the foregoing stupor were in vain. The distraction of his obsession was severely inculcated in his mind. Therefore, unable to concentrate on the prayers of the rosary, the youth now beseeched the Almighty to rescue him from his madness.

Overhead, meanwhile, a flock of five vultures flew. Just as they had flown two days beforehand, the fowl again floated, glided, careened, and soared. Having gathered, they then circled directly over the trudging Mexican boy. Soon, they would begin to gravitate toward him in corkscrew swirls.

Lazarillo was growing faint with vertigo. Desperately, he searched the corners of his mind, attempting to rediscover something or some point of reference on which he could anchor his thoughts and thereby save himself from his insanity. Hope was now granted, as we shall see.

There came to the youngster's recollection a special prayer which he had learned from his maternal grandmother. He remembered how she would recite it to him at bedtime. It was the *Memorare*, a prayer to the Blessed Mother.

Since he hadn't heard or recited the prayer for several years, a time which had lapsed since his grandmother's death, it was necessary for him to do some mind-mapping so he could reconstruct the prayer and recite it with meaning. The foregoing recall was, in itself, therapeutic for the lad. Almost immediately, his obsession to conjure the familiar images in his brain was replaced by an unrelenting zeal to rediscover something meaningful and positive. He then remembered how his grandmother would kneel down at the right side of his bed; and, while covering his forehead, she would recite the prayer. This translates into English in the following way:

"Remember, oh most gracious Virgin Mary, never was it known that anyone who fled to Your protection, implored Your help, or sought Your intercession was left unaided. Inspired by this confidence, I call to You, oh Virgin of Virgins, my Lady! To You I go, and before You I stand, contrite and sorrowful. Oh, sweet Mother of the Word Incarnate, reject *not* my petition but HEAR AND ASWER ME! Amen."

Upon finishing his evocation, there occurred an incident of a singular kind, one that affected the boy and all other things animate and inanimate. A darkness, universal so it seemed, blanketed everything. Confounded by the phenomenon, *Lazarillo* stopped in his tracks and remained standing in place. Next, a bright light shone before him. Refulgent, it forced him to close his eyes and cover them with the palms of his hands. All the while, he kept the rosary wrapped around his right hand. The current incandescence was overwhelming, so much so that the boy humbly dropped to his knees as if he was preparing to pray some more. It was then that he heard the gentle voice of a woman:

"Come to me, my love. Nestle your weary head. I will give you rest and protection. My love for you is great and everlasting. Come, be not afraid, oh sweet child of mine. Leave your cares and woes behind you. Surrender your heart to me. I will heal and cherish it. I want you. You are very special to me. Trust in me, *Lazarillo*. I am your Mother. Look up and you shall see."

Having raised his head, the Mexican peasant saw a sight to behold. It was that of the Madonna, the Mother of God! The apparition was irrefutably the most sublime of the boy's life. Spellbound, he gazed at Her and saw a woman of extraordinary beauty.

Standing on a fluffy white cloud, the Virgin descended slowly and gracefully. As She approached the Mexican boy, Her countenance, shape, and indumentum evinced themselves to him. A veil of satin, colored aqua, was anchored firmly on the Virgin's head by a gilded crown. Draping downward, it covered the shoulders and backside. A dress of white satin, one that contrasted with Her very bronze complexion, was cinched to Her trim waist by a gilded cord. This was knotted in a bow about two inches above the umbilicus. Her abdomen, slightly plump, contracted and expanded with each breath she took. Breasts, firm but delicate, likened to those of a maiden.

On the Lady's veil, as well as on her dress, pleats rippled commensurately with the contours and movements of Her graceful body. Said dress, hemmed at the bottom, covered the torso, legs, and feet, but not the toes. These protruded from sandals made of gilded cloth.

Hair, as black as the night during a quarter moon's phase, very visibly undulated and unfurled upon the Madonna's shoulders and therefore contrasted, in color, with Her dress of a Eucharistic white. Every aspect of the Virgin's countenance was symmetrically perfect and proportionate to Her head. A nose protruded slightly between two eyes of glassy onyx. Lashes and eye brows resembled those of a Barbie doll. Cheeks dimpled near a noble chin when She smiled, and as She spoke to the young peasant, Her mouth opened and closed placidly while well-chosen words flowed from a pair of delicate lips.

"Come to me, my brave young man!" Invited the Virgin.

Dazzled by Her brilliance, and captivated by the beauty which She radiated, the young Mexican threw himself head first at the Lady's feet. Then, wrapping his arms around Her ankles, he lay prostrate. As he hugged the foregoing body parts, a torrential flow of tears burst forth from his eyes and onto the Virgin's feet! Sobbing so, he trembled! Soon, the sobs were accompanied by a spasmodic shuddering! Trembling, he seemed to be begging Her caress!

Bending gracefully at the knees, the Madonna stooped downward and placed the palms of her gentle hands on each side of the lad's head. Soothing was the touch. Kneeling down, She then positioned Her posterior on Her Achilles tendons, and thereby created a comfortable cushion on Her lap for the youngster's head as he lay.

Curling up in a fetal position, the youth placed the left side of his head on the Virgin's lap. At the same time, he removed his arms from Her ankles and wrapped them around Her delicate waist. In doing so, he felt his face sink into Her plump abdomen. While remaining in this position, he continued to cry frenetically! As the boy cried, he clung to The Chosen One like a child clings to a mother after experiencing a nightmare!

Eventually, *Lazarillo* 's sobs became sorrowful moans and groans, ones that emanated not from the vocal chords but from the entrails! It was as if centuries of repressed rancor, one that had been bequeathed to him by his progenitors, was now manifesting itself! Gushing forth with geyser-like force, it flowed from deep down within an area where the malignity had festered for too long a time! Contractions, functioning autonomously inside his stomach wall, were repelling and ejecting that vile-fetid bile which had accumulated! Yes, human injustices were those which had culminated into a gigantic heap of rancid and decrepit waste, the stench of which would have offended life's lowest form of scum!

All the while, the poor lad trembled feverishly; and, while keeping his eyes shut, he pressed his face against the soft protruding plumpness of the Virgin's ventral wall! His movements were like those of a newborn kitten, which, not having yet received the gift of sight, pokes its face persistently and aimlessly against the mother's breast and attempts to locate the source of nourishment.

The foregoing catharsis finally drew to a close, and the peasant boy, drained of every bit of energy, fell into a deep sleep. Having relaxed every muscle in his body, he lay limp, with his head buried in the Lady's lap. Reminiscent was the scene of *La Pietà*, the statue of the Blessed Mother holding the lifeless body of Jesus in her lap.

Daylight was now miraculously restored, and the mid-afternoon sun shone brightly over the sea of tassels once more.

A helicopter, sweeping over the carpet of said tassels, halted in mid air and hovered over the spot on the ground where *Lazarillo* lay. Thither, the aforementioned vultures were beginning to descend upon him. The pilot of the helicopter, having caught sight of the scene, decided to intervene. In the cockpit, his voice could be heard as he communicated, in broken English, to his dispatcher:

"Unita wonne to da dispacha. Comma inne, pleeza."

"This is dispatch. Go ahead, United One."

"I seea body inna da corna field. Looka lika *Messicano* boya. I droppa downa anna taka looka."

"What's your ten-twenty?" Asked the dispatcher.

"Imma justa finisha witte Henry's field." Answered the pilot.

"Remember, *DiAngelo,* you still have to dust Haddock's crop!" Ordered the dispatcher. And then, the dialogue between dispatcher and pilot proceeded.

"I knowa. Butta day say isa gonna raina anyway. So, I dusta anotha daya. No usa dusta nowa. Raina gonna wash everyting awaya. Farmer loosa da money, you knowa."

"That's tough shit!" Said the dispatcher. "I don't care if he loses his mother! Haddock already paid big bucks for a dusting, and he'll get what he paid for! If the rain washes away the insecticides, he can pay for another dusting!"

"Well, ahmma gonna dropa downa anyway." Said the pilot.

"You listen to me, wop! Do as I say or go back to living with your *spaghetti*-bending *paisanos!*" Then he added. "You do want your green card, don't you?"

"Whata you saya? I no copy. Too mucha noise, too much statica!" Said *DiAngelo.*

"Why, you dumb fuckin' dago, no good guinea son of a bitch!"

"I no copy! Unita wonne, ten-seven! I droppa downa anna helpa da *Messicano* boya!"

DiAngelo's radio clicked, as he signaled out. Immediately afterward, he maneuvered the helicopter to a spot about seventy yards above where *Lazarillo* lay.

Curled up in a fetal position while lying on his left side, the young peasant was embracing the base of a corn stalk. His face was nestled in a plump mound, one that usually forms around the base of a plant, precisely where the latter meets the ground.

The buzzards, meanwhile, had landed on a rather large piece of driftwood that was strewn on the road's shoulder, not far from the irrigation ditch. Thither they sat perched. Eagerly waiting for the boy to expire, they repeatedly positioned and repositioned themselves on the log.

What usually transpired in similar instances, one could easily imagine. For example, after the subject expired, each of the vultures would vie over choice portions of the cadaver. First, they would attack the stomach, the buttocks, and the genitals! Subsequently, they would peck at the heart and eyes! The rest would be left for insects, rodents, and crows!

Viewed from the airborne chopper, the boy's reclining body likened to a sketch on the ground, the kind that is made by policemen to outline the spot and position of a fallen victim of a suicide or homicide.

The chopper now careened, swerved, and descended gradually over an area not far from the shoulder of the highway where the vultures sat perched on the piece of driftwood. Alarmed by the intrusion, the birds took to flight. Retaining their curiosity, they alighted nearby, in a location where they could keep a watchful eye on their prey and observe the helicopter as well.

Descending, the craft and its propeller sent gusty winds that ruffled every cornstalk within a thirty-five-yard radius from where it was beginning to alight! As soon as the chopper touched ground, the pilot's door flung open and a corpulent man burst out of the cockpit! Hopping across the irrigation ditch, he dashed through the cornfield to the spot where the Mexican boy lay! *Di Angelo's* thrust likened to that of a raging bull, one that dashes out into the arena after the corral door is raised!

Having sped through the cornfield, the Italian soon reached *Lazarillo*. Bending over, he took the boy in his arms. Then, trudging along the rugged ground, he attempted to save the lad from the hungry predators who had been watching the scene from where they hid.

Upset by the intrusion, the vultures quickly sallied forth and attacked *DiAngelo*. First, the five of them took turns pecking at his back and buttocks! Next, they aimed at the man's stomach and genitals, obtrusively attempting to intimidate him so that he would abandon his mission!

Outraged by the birds' audacity, the Italian decided to retaliate. First, he gently lay the boy supine in a furrow. Then, he reached for the piece of driftwood upon which the buzzards had perched; and, grasping it at the narrower of its two ends with both hands, he wielded it savagely in a number of directions! Imitating the movements of an athlete in a hammer throw event, he proceeded to swing the log repeatedly from right to left and from left to right! By doing so, he managed to make contact with the wing of one of the vultures. Injured, the latter scampered off like a turkey attempting to eschew a butcher.

In the meantime, the Italian struck another buzzard. Smashing it on the back, he succeeded in crippling the creature! Immobilized, the bird lay on its backside. In its eyes was the look of someone beseeching an executioner to have mercy.

Notwithstanding the vulture's plea, *DiAngelo* felt the self-righteousness of the Archangel, who, according to the Bible, drove Lucifer and his cohorts out of heaven. Thus, continuing to hold the piece of driftwood at one end, he raised it above his head, and, like a merciless executioner, he delivered the final *coup de grâce!* Consumed with anger, he repeated the foregoing process over and over until the bird's brains, eyes, and intestines oozed and quivered as they were violently crushed and bashed by a brutal clubbing from the battling pilot!

Having ridded the area of his opposition, the Italian rushed to the spot where *Lazarillo* was lying! Upon arriving there, he took the wrist of the lad's right hand and searched for a pulse. Nothing! Next, the man with a mission tore open the boy's shirt at the chest, and, employing both hands, he tried to resuscitate the youth by applying pressure to the thoracic cavity and massaging the heart. Still no sign of life!

In the atmosphere, meanwhile, a sweeping gust of wind invasively blew over the land like a *scirocco* blows over the African desert and into the Mediterranean! Clouds then began to clutter the sky. Ominous, they announced a foreboding of doom and destruction!

The rescuer acted quickly. Taking the boy in his arms, he carried him to the helicopter the way in which a shepherd carries a wounded lamb to shelter. Upon reaching the craft, the Italian opened the door to the passenger side and gently deposited the lad on the floor directly behind the pilot's seat. Thereat, he secured the body with safety belts.

Time-wise, it was about three o'clock in the afternoon. By then, the cloud formation had grown and thickened. Grayish-black, it hovered in the troposphere like a colossal blanket and created the ambience of a ubiquitous dusk. At the same time, an atmospheric pressure weighed heavily overhead and caused a certain uneasiness among all living things thereabout. One could say that the current moment was the quiet before the storm.

Lightening soon struck the heavens and illuminated the entire desert. So bright was the incandescence that it almost completely restored the daylight which had been suppressed by the dark storm clouds.

Then, a resounding boom thundered! This was followed by a torrential downpour. Hailstones, the size of marbles, so they seemed, thrashed the chopper's exterior shell! And for several moments to come, intermittent series of bolts and booms erupted whilst the pilot prepared to launch!

Having made sure that *Lazarillo* was secured in place, *DiAngelo* jumped, butt first, into the pilot's seat. Sitting at the controls, he flipped on various switches and started the engine. As a result of his actions, a sonorous whirring noise resounded! Next, the distinctive chopping din ensued while the overhead prop proceeded to spin in the wind! Seizing the control stick with his right hand, the pilot now pulled back. In doing so, he caused the chopper to launch and readily take to flight.

The helicopter proceeded to climb, notwithstanding the adverse weather conditions. Ascending, it might rise above the blanket of clouds, thought the pilot, whence he could chart a course that would take him and his passenger to safety. Such was his hope.

In the meantime, hurricane-force winds and torrential rains combined to make navigation almost impossible! Indeed, the chopper bobbed up and down, and it swayed from one side to the other before soaring upward and then downward, losing altitude as rapidly as a roller coaster in a downward thrust! Under such conditions, the coaster tends to fall rapidly, thereby giving the passengers a terrifying sense of helplessness and insecurity. Then, just when stomachs adjust to the descent, the coaster abruptly soars upward, leaving the passengers with hearts in their mouths!

The tempestuousness seemed inescapable. Every time the pilot attempted to steer the craft in a particular direction in order to correct his being thrown off course, he would be violently tossed into another. As a matter of fact, the only direction over which *Di Angelo* seemed to have any measure of control was an upward one. Accordingly, he seized that control stick again and yanked it all the way back to his knees. At the same time, he placed the throttle at maximum velocity.

Gaining altitude, the chopper trembled as its engine strained! Whirring all the more, its powerful prop churned in an attempt to defy gravity and weather the elements as well! Soon, said engine broke into a vitriolic whine! So obstreperous was the din, that had it continued, an explosion would have been imminent! Meanwhile, bolts and rivets rattled while windows and doors shook! Then, suddenly, the helicopter's bottom caught a sweeping turbulence of wind which propelled its entire shell into space without need of the engine! Soaring with a force that likened to jet propulsion, the craft's destiny was completely out of the pilot's control and in the hands of an authority greater than he! Indeed, continuing to gain altitude, the flying machine bore a semblance to a space craft, one that was being propelled into another galaxy!

During the event described above, the Virgin Mary prepared to take leave of *Lazarillo*. Her words were promising; their tone, soothing: "It's time to wake up, my brave young man. You'll be safe now. Remember, dear, that I love you. I will love you unconditionally forever. I must go now, my love, but my spirit will remain in your heart and in your soul."

Lazarillo exclaimed: "No! No! Don't leave me! I need you! I don't want to be alone anymore! Please don't go away!"

As he pleaded with the Lady, he tightened his grip on Her. Then, She proceeded to talk: "You will never be alone, my Son. Your Father will watch over you, and I will do the same. Your family and your people need you, my love. Love them the way I love you."

Upon finishing Her last statement to the young peasant, the Madonna bent over, and, placing Her hands on each side of his face, She gently guided his body upward so that he stood face to face with Her. Then, She gently kissed the youth on the forehead.

All of a sudden, the helicopter's cabin lit up, as if a massive bolt of lightening had struck it! A moment afterwards, moreover, the chopper's engine ceased straining and its shell sailed gracefully in the heavens, like a ship sails calmly in a safe haven. All was calm. All was bright.

Lazarillo attempted to raise himself, but the belts that girded his body prevented him from doing so. While he struggled with the belts, he also felt the urge to cover his eyes with both hands and to rub them, as one does when going from pitch darkness to light. Such was the intensity of the sudden coruscation.

The pilot, using both hands as well, also shielded his eyes from the current brilliance. And, when he sensed his sights were adapted, he uncovered them and glanced straight ahead into the windshield. The wraparound feature of the latter provided him with an all-encompassing view of what lay ahead, below, above, and on each side of the craft.

How spectacular the panorama! About seventy feet below the copter, white, fleece-like clouds, an unending blanket of them, covered the land. The sky above was of an azure coloration, and the post-meridian glow of the sun smiled at the vessel as this cruised toward it with the ease of a chariot that was carrying chosen souls to paradise.

While staring at the view, *DiAngelo* heard a voice call out from behind him, "No! Don't leave me! I don't want to be alone anymore!" Then, there was a moan and a few questions: "What is this? Where am I? Where did She go?"

The Italian, assured of being in control of his craft, put the engine on automatic pilot, and, freeing himself from his safety belt, he turned around to his right and left the cockpit in order to attend to *Lazarillo*. While kneeling down alongside the youth, he proceeded to undo the belts which secured his body. Meanwhile, the youngster stared spellbound at his rescuer and attempted to identify him.

"Who are you? What am I doing here? What happened to the Lady?" Asked the boy. While making inquiries, he studied the individual who had rescued him.

There was something regal about the man's countenance. A nose, Roman shaped, protruded from an olive-complexioned face and separated a pair of dark brown eyes. These were staring with no little intensity. Hair, black and curly, unfurled onto the Italian's brow and temples like waves of the Tyrrhenian Sea, which, flowing gracefully toward the land, cover its sun-blessed shores. Moreover, a stubble for a beard shadowed a pair of prominent cheeks, an upper lip, and a distinguished chin.

"Ahma da *pilotto* fo da *elicottero*." Replied *DiAngelo*. Then, he added. "Ahma dusta da corna fiieldsa."

"Where did She go? Why did She leave me"? Repeated the youth. *DiAngelo* responded: "Ah no see nobody here, justa you anda meah."

After a few seconds, the pilot asked, "Whatsa you nama, kid?" *Lazarillo* answered, and then the pilot explained how he had found the boy lifeless in one of the cornfields and that he endeavored to fly the boy to a hospital.

Next, the man exclaimed, "Ah tella you, eeza *miracolo!* Wonne minute you wasa dead, and da nexta minute you is aliva! *Mamma mia!*"

Meanwhile, at the chopper's control panel, a red, button-shaped light was blinking on and off. This activity was accompanied by a noticeable buzzing noise, the kind that acts as a warning device.

"Accidente al demonio!"

Complained the Italian in his native tongue. Then he added, "Eeza da warning fo da fuel! Tank eeza almosta empty!"

Wasting no time, the pilot returned to his seat in a flash. *Lazarillo,* almost simultaneously, dashed for the one on the passenger side. The pilot then checked the fuel gauge. Sure enough. The chopper was low on fuel. Estimated flying time was about ten or fifteen minutes at most.

Both man and boy now gazed straight ahead in an attempt to get a bearing as to their present location. However, blinded by the glare of the late noon's sun, they immediately glanced downward. The following is what met their eyes.

No more clouds. Instead, mountains, many of them, and not too few knolls bulged from the earth's network of valleys, gorges, and ravines. Moistened by the recent storm which had passed, the earth appeared fertile and fresh. Of a shady green coloration, it was wanting of the light from a waning solar glow. Streams, meanwhile, bubbling from the earth's higher elevations, trickled down mountain sides. Joining one another, they formed rivers which worked their way serpentinuously downward, constantly seeking the level of the sea.

Continuing to view the foregoing topography, pilot and passenger perceived something that brought them hope. Houses, clusters of them, populated one of the aforementioned valleys. Colored white, the structures readily manifested themselves in contrast to the dark green coloration of the terrain. This, by the way, abounded in open areas where aircraft could easily land.

Pushing forward on the control stick, the pilot caused the chopper to nose toward land.

"Holda onna ma boy! We gonna landa!" Urged the pilot.

The craft's front end dipped considerably, so much so that it was headed for the clusters of houses at an angle of about ninety degrees. Having neared them, *DiAngelo* yanked back on the control stick so that his chopper flew about fifty yards over the structures.

While combing the area in the foregoing manner, the pilot had noticed a fueling station on the east side of town. Hence, doubling back, he caused the craft to hover over said station before landing in an open spot which had a pump with access for aircraft and diesel trucks. *DiAngelo* maneuvered the helicopter so that its right side was accessible to the pump. He then got out of the craft, removed the gasoline cap, and proceeded to fuel. After filling the tank, the pilot put the cap back on and returned the pump to its former position. Next, he paid the attendant and then attended to some personal matters.

The two voyagers used the station's toilet facilities, and then they walked around the open area of the fueling station in order to stretch their legs and breathe some fresh air. After ten minutes or so, both of them returned to their seats in the chopper's cockpit.

The day's late rays were now peeking through the port side of the copter's glassy cockpit. Intense was the gleam. As a result, the pilot used his hands to shade his eyes as he gazed at the western heavens. What he saw was a familiar scene, one that we frequently see at the end of a day, particularly after a storm has passed.

Fleecy clusters of white clouds hung motionless and cluttered a firmament of turquoise blue. In the meantime, solar beams streamed from the setting sun's upper quarter, and a jagged range of mountain tops silhouetted against the illuminated sky. Some of the foregoing beams appeared refracted by the fluffy cloud clusters. Others, uninterrupted by the nebulae, extended throughout the turquoise background, whereupon hues of a pinkish-peach coloration meshed and blended. So delicate were the soft tinctures of the heavens that it seemed as if they had been gently dabbed or smudged thereon by the light, agile strokes of an able artist's hand. Delicate and colorful, the tinges served to additionally embellish a relishing rapture of celestial beauty. Divine was the scene! Heavenly, indeed, it likened to a fresco by the famed Michelangelo!

In the cockpit, the Italian reached for a bag that was behind his seat. Drawing it to his lap, he inserted his right hand in that receptacle and extracted an entire loaf of bread. Then, he tore off a generous portion from one of the loaf's ends and gave it to *Lazarillo*. Afterwards, he did the same for himself. Famished, the two of them ate with great pleasure, and while doing so, they discussed plans. The Italian initiated the conversation.

" So, where you wanna go now, kid?"

"Home, to see my mother. Can you take me there?"

"I willa try." Then, the pilot asked, "Where you liva?"

The youngster gestured with his right hand. "Over there, on the east side."

"Shoulda be no problem." Replied the pilot.

Having finished the snack, pilot and passenger fastened their safety belts. Next, a whirring sound wound as DiAngelo turned on the engine. The chopper's propellers then churned once again. Within seconds, the craft began its ascent.

As the chopper flew away from the sun, *DiAngelo* and *Lazarillo* gazed straight ahead in the direction where heavenly shades of night were starting to fall. Watching, they saw a full moon that was hovering above the high Sierras. Soon, they would see it begin to journey over the ocean of verdure.

Gaping downward, then, man and boy saw an infinity of tassel-tipped talks unravel about fifty yards beneath them. Moistened by the recent downpour, the vegetation appeared fresh and green to the eyes of the gazers.

Within about twenty minutes from take off, the voyagers passed over the highway, the one which ran down the center of the valley. Traffic was scarce on the thoroughfare at that moment in time, and the vehicles that were observed by the two surveyors had their lights turned on. Dim, at present, the headlights' glow would grow commensurately with the crepuscular phase to which we have alluded above.

Here and there, crews of pickers were viewed by the Italian and his companion. While both of them focused their attention on the crewmembers that were amidst the jungle of verdure, they noticed that the individuals formicated alongside a tractor-towed bin. Moreover, watching them repetitively step and bend, then shuck and chuck, they saw those crewmembers fill the tractor-towed bins with freshly picked ears of corn.

For the Mexican peasant, that experience was completely unprecedented. Looking downward, he watched the stalks bend like palm trees in a storm as the craft swept over the patches of crop-filled plots. And, in addition to viewing the aforementioned crews of pickers, the boy also saw jackrabbits buoyantly spring from furrow to furrow. Coons, moreover, met the boy's eyes as he gazed in awe. Peering, he saw them scour furrows for viands. Continuing to watch them, he saw the burly beasts gather vitals and bring them to nearby canals for a cleansing. The boy also set sights on a coyote. All fours planted at the bank of a canal, the canine visibly licked and lapped the liquid at the waterway's shore. A mountain lion soon entered the scene. Dauntingly, it crept through the jungle of stalks in search of prey.

All of the creatures listed hereinabove winced with no little vigor as the clamorous chopper flew overhead.

All of a sudden, the pilot exclaimed, "Whatsa dat ova dere?" He pointed straight ahead at a spot about three miles in the distance. Lights yonder, some electric and others from oven fires, sparkled in the early evening hour.

"*¡Es mi pueblo!*" Exclaimed the lad.

Yes, the youngster's town lay yonder. Nestled in the foothills of the Sierra, it wasn't but a camptown, one that was similar to the group of shacks we observed at the beginning of our story. Shanties, about thirteen of them, were constructed in a circle which surrounded a well. Drab and worn, the shacks belched with the same impoverished condition we have already observed.

While the helicopter drew nigh to the huts, its engine's noise and the props caused a commotion thereabout. Men, women, and children burst from their homes in order to discover the cause for such a ruckus. Petrified, they remained at their thresholds, but dared not advance beyond them.

Meanwhile, the chopper hovered above the shantytown's circular configuration, and then it gradually alighted and landed near the aforementioned well.

As the craft touched ground, *Lazarillo* flung open its door and dashed to a shack where a woman and two children were standing!

Laying eyes on her son, the woman cried out, "...¡M'hijo! ¡M'hijo! ¡Gracias a Dios!

Mother and son raced toward each other. Then, the woman threw her arms around the lad, and the two of them embraced. So tender was the scene! Just imagine the two of them reunited, after so much worry and grief.

Soon, *Lazarillo's* younger brother and sister got into the act. In unison, the four of them clung to each other as the family dog jumped and tugged at them with his paws while yelping, barking, and whining.

DiAngelo, having remained in the chopper, was concerned about having disobeyed his supervisor. Accordingly, he attempted to call dispatch in order to attempt a reconciliation.

"Unita wonne to da dispatch. Comma ina, please."

The following was the supervisor's response: "You motherfuckin' son of a bitchin' dago! You get that chopper back to base ASAP or I'm gonna be all over you like a fly on a turd!"

To which *DiAngelo* replied: "You cana taka you *elicottero* anda you joba anda stickem upa you ass." Then, a terse click ensued and the pilot went 10-7.

After signing off, the Italian opened the helicopter door to his side. Then, brusquely jumping out and on to the earth, he approached the jubilant family and joined in their celebration.

Upon seeing the Italian, *Lazarillo's* mother and two younger children were astonished. He wasn't exactly like them, they noticed; yet at the same time, they all felt a certain commonality.

Lazarillo took the initiative and introduced *DiAngelo* to his family. Moreover, he explained how the Italian saved his life.

The mother thanked the man from the bottom of her heart, and then she invited him to stay with them. He accepted.

Twilight was beginning to invade the ambience. Overhead, meanwhile, the full moon and a multitude of stars were already reflecting a faint solar light which glowed in the western horizon. Colored reddish-gold, the foregoing glimmer likened to smoldering logs in the hearth of a quaint country home. Pleasing to the eyes, it was an omen of tranquility and well-being. A silence, broken only by the creaking of crickets, complemented the peace that reigned in the valley. Meanwhile, an appetizing odor of oven baked *tortillas* and refried beans filled the air as *DiAngelo* followed the family and all entered the humble abode.

The End